Jon
Stewart

Other books in the People in the News series:

Maya Angelou

Tyra Banks

Glenn Beck

David Beckham

Beyoncé

Sandra Bullock

Fidel Castro

Kelly Clarkson

Hillary Clinton

Miley Cyrus

Ellen Degeneres

Johnny Depp

Leonardo DiCaprio

Hilary Duff

Zac Efron

Brett Favre

50 Cent

Jeff Gordon

Al Gore

Tony Hawk

Salma Hayek

Jennifer Hudson

LeBron James

Jay-Z

Derek Jeter

Steve Jobs

Dwayne Johnson

Angelina Jolie

Jonas Brothers

Kim Jong II

Coretta Scott King

Ashton Kutcher

Spike Lee

George Lopez

Tobey Maguire

Eli Manning

John McCain

Barack Obama

Michelle Obama

Apolo Anton Ohno

Danica Patrick

Nancy Pelosi

Katy Perry

Tyler Perry

Queen Latifah

Daniel Radcliffe

Condoleezza Rice

Rihanna

Alex Rodriguez

Derrick Rose

J.K. Rowling

Shakira

Tupac Shakur

Will Smith

Gwen Stefani

Ben Stiller

Hilary Swank

Justin Timberlake

Usher

Denzel Washington

Serena Williams

Oprah Winfrey

32858   4/8/13

Jon
Stewart

by Randy Scherer

LUCENT BOOKS
A part of Gale, Cengage Learning

GALE
CENGAGE Learning

Detroit • New York • San Francisco • New Haven, Conn • Waterville, Maine • London

GALE
CENGAGE Learning™

LIBRARY OF CONGRESS CATALOGING-IN-PUBLICATION DATA

Scherer, Randy.
  Jon Stewart / by Randy Scherer.
    p. cm. -- (People in the news)
  Includes bibliographical references and index.
  ISBN 978-1-4205-0608-2 (hardcover)
1. Stewart, Jon, 1962- 2. Comedians--United States--Biography. 3. Actors--
United States--Biography. 4. Television personalities--United States--Biography. I. Title.
  PN2287.S683S35 2011
  792.702'8092--dc23
  [B]
                                                                    2011023802

Lucent Books
27500 Drake Rd
Farmington Hills MI 48331

ISBN-13: 978-1-4205-0608-2
ISBN-10: 1-4205-0608-0

Contents

Fame and celebrity are alluring. People are drawn to those who walk in fame's spotlight, whether they are known for great accomplishments or for notorious deeds. The lives of the famous pique public interest and attract attention, perhaps because their experiences seem in some ways so different from, yet in other ways so similar to, our own.

Newspapers, magazines, and television regularly capitalize on this fascination with celebrity by running profiles of famous people. For example, television programs such as *Entertainment Tonight* devote all their programming to stories about entertainment and entertainers. Magazines such as *People* fill their pages with stories of the private lives of famous people. Even newspapers, newsmagazines, and television news frequently delve into the lives of well-known personalities. Despite the number of articles and programs, few provide more than a superficial glimpse at their subjects.

Lucent's People in the News series offers young readers a deeper look into the lives of today's newsmakers, the influences that have shaped them, and the impact they have had in their fields of endeavor and on other people's lives. The subjects of the series hail from many disciplines and walks of life. They include authors, musicians, athletes, political leaders, entertainers, entrepreneurs, and others who have made a mark on modern life and who, in many cases, will continue to do so for years to come.

These biographies are more than factual chronicles. Each book emphasizes the contributions, accomplishments, or deeds that have brought fame or notoriety to the individual and shows how that person has influenced modern life. Authors portray their subjects in a realistic, unsentimental light. For example, Bill Gates—cofounder of the software giant Microsoft—has been instrumental in making personal computers the most vital tool of the modern age. Few dispute his business savvy, his perseverance, or his technical expertise, yet critics say he is ruthless in his dealings with competitors and driven more by his desire to maintain Microsoft's dominance in the computer industry than by an interest in furthering technology.

In these books, young readers will encounter inspiring stories about real people who achieved success despite enormous obstacles. Oprah Winfrey—one of the most powerful, most watched, and wealthiest women in television history—spent the first six years of her life in the care of her grandparents while her unwed mother sought work and a better life elsewhere. Her adolescence was colored by pregnancy at age fourteen, rape, and sexual abuse.

Each author documents and supports his or her work with an array of primary and secondary source quotations taken from diaries, letters, speeches, and interviews. All quotes are footnoted to show readers exactly how and where biographers derive their information and provide guidance for further research. The quotations enliven the text by giving readers eyewitness views of the life and accomplishments of each person covered in the People in the News series.

In addition, each book in the series includes photographs, annotated bibliographies, timelines, and comprehensive indexes. For both the casual reader and the student researcher, the People in the News series offers insight into the lives of today's newsmakers—people who shape the way we live, work, and play in the modern age.

From News Mocker to News Maker

What does it mean to be the most trusted name in fake news? For Jon Stewart, the comedian who hosts Comedy Central's half-hour news and entertainment program *The Daily Show*, it means being able to access America's most powerful politicians, carve out a respected place as a thoughtful media critic, and become one of the most trusted voices in current events. Indeed, after more than a decade as *The Daily Show's* host, Stewart has gone from mocking the news to making it.

How did Stewart grow from a little-known late night comic to one of the most powerful voices in the media? "I wish I could say there was a magic formula," he says, "but I just kept working at it."[1]

A Social Commentator Is Born

Like many comedians, talk show hosts, and comedy writers, Stewart began his career as a struggling stand-up comedian in the New York City comedy club circuit. He moved on to a variety of short-lived shows and had minor parts in mainly unsuccessful movies. He eventually hit his stride as the host of *The Daily Show with Jon Stewart* in January 1999. Just a year later, Stewart and his staff won one of the most prestigious awards in television, the Peabody Award for excellence in radio and television broadcasting, for their satirical coverage of the 2000 U.S. presidential election.

Jon Stewart tapes an episode of his award-winning program,
The Daily Show with Jon Stewart. *During his time on
the show, the former stand-up comedian has become an
influential social and political commentator.*

Under Stewart's direction, *The Daily Show* has found its "magic
formula," which involves using multimedia clips, a team of
correspondents, and Stewart's own comedic voice to highlight

both the absurdity and hypocrisy of politics and the mainstream media's coverage of current events. As he puts it, "We function as a sort of editorial cartoon."[2] However, Stewart's cartoons do not appear in any newspaper, but rather offer a fast-paced mix of multimedia and comedic commentary.

In turn, Stewart has become an influential news maker and social commentator himself. For example, Stewart made news in 2004 when he went on CNN's program *Crossfire* to criticize it. Two months later the network president said he agreed with Stewart's criticisms, and he canceled the show and fired one of the hosts. Stewart has also taken aim at campaign journalists, the Fox News Channel and its many personalities, the financial news network CNBC, and countless politicians. Each time, Stewart and *The Daily Show* blend carefully edited bits of media with satirical commentary to reveal bias, hypocrisy, and even stupidity in American politics and media coverage.

In Stewart America Trusts

Through his mock newscasts, satirical books, a Rally to Restore Sanity and/or Fear that drew over two hundred thousand people to Washington, D.C., and even advocacy that helped get legislation for 9/11 first responders passed, Stewart's focus on using comedy to discuss current events and the media has earned him his audience's trust. In fact, after famous journalist Walter Cronkite passed away in 2009, *Time* magazine asked its readers whom they most trusted for the news—and Stewart topped a list of traditional journalists, beating out Brian Williams, Charlie Gibson, and Katie Couric for the honor.

By all accounts Stewart has carved out a niche for himself and won the respect of his industry. In addition to the two Peabody Awards his show won for its presidential election coverage, in twelve years with Stewart as the host of *The Daily Show*, he and his team have won fourteen Emmy Awards in a number of categories for comedy or variety shows. Stewart's recording of an audio book won a Grammy Award, and he and his show have won individual and group awards for both comedy and news from the Television

Critics Association—further emphasizing Stewart's unique ability to straddle the line between news and entertainment.

Stewart has earned these awards for his accomplishments in taking the timeless art of political satire into the multimedia, Internet age. The result is a clever and hilarious blend of comedy mixed with astute observations, scathing criticism, and even, at times, investigative exposé. "Many of us on this side of the journalism tracks often wish we were on Jon's side," comments NBC news anchor and regular *Daily Show* guest Brian Williams. "I envy his platform to shout from the mountaintop. He's a necessary branch of government."[3]

Staying Outside the Game

It is widely agreed that Stewart is a skilled comedian and satirist. But his real talent might be the way in which he toes the line between satire and seriousness, comedy and journalism, and advocacy and criticism. Stewart stays in the middle of these extremes, careful to stay outside of many of the industries on which he comments. This allows him to criticize and joke freely, without attachment, and separate from what he calls "the game." "I could have gotten on the field. And people got mad that I didn't," he once told MSNBC television host Rachel Maddow. "That's my failing. And my indulgence. But I feel like I am where I belong."[4]

Although Stewart has received awards typically given to journalists, is trusted by many in the public for their news, and is respected by his peers in the media, he insists that he is just trying to be a good comedian, and that means getting the story right. "We don't do anything but make the connections," Stewart has said. "We don't fact check [and] look at context because of any *journalistic* criteria that has to be met. We do that because jokes don't work when they're lies. We fact-check so when we tell a joke, it hits you at sort of a gut level — not because we have a journalistic integrity, [but because] hopefully we have a comedic integrity that we don't want to violate."[5] In truth, Stewart's efforts to do well in comedy have led him to be a leading voice in news and politics, which is nothing to laugh at.

Chapter 1

The Little Kid Who Got Big Laughs

Jon Stewart was born Jonathan Stuart Leibowitz in a New York City hospital on November 28, 1962. His family lived in the small suburban town of Lawrenceville, New Jersey. Jon's father, Donald Leibowitz, worked as a physicist at RCA Laboratories in nearby Princeton. Jon's mother, Marian Laskin Leibowitz, was first a special education teacher and then an educational consultant.

A Childhood with Few Complaints

Jon and his older brother, Larry, enjoyed a mostly happy childhood. Their family was a fairly typical representation of the Jewish population in the New York metropolitan area in that they were well educated and middle-class. Nathan Laskin, Marian's father—Jon's grandfather—had owned a series of small fur shops and lived for a period in Tianjin, China. Marian remembers her father as a very funny man. In fact, he performed in nightclubs in China for extra money when he was young. As a child Jon enjoyed spending time with his grandfather and felt especially close to him. On his father's side, his grandfather had been a cab driver in New York City and was part of a religious family.

Although there were not many Jewish families in the neighborhood in which Jon grew up, he did attend a Jewish kindergarten called a yeshiva. In first grade he joined his brother at the local public

Funnyman Stewart first began making people laugh as a young boy, when he used humor as a way to fit in with his classmates.

school. Jon remembers occasionally being teased by other children because he was Jewish. He was also teased because he was smaller than his classmates. One of the ways in which he coped was making people laugh. "I was very little, so being funny helped me have big friends,"[6] he says. Jon soon discovered he liked the attention he got from making people laugh.

Despite occasionally being bullied by the neighborhood kids, Jon had more friends than enemies. He describes his childhood as happy and somewhat ordinary:

> My life was typical. I played a little Little League baseball. I never wanted for food. I always had shoes. I had a room. There were no great tragedies. There were the typical ups and downs but I wouldn't say it was at all sad. We were Jewish and living in the suburbs so there was a slightly neurotic bent to it, but I can't point to anything where a boy overcame a tragedy to become a comedian. As my grandmother used to say, "I can't complain."[7]

In addition to Little League baseball, Jon also played soccer. He and his friends used to play at the fields at the local community college. "It would be 20 degrees out and the ground would be frozen solid, and we would be out there running around like idiots,"[8] he remembers.

Although he enjoyed playing outdoors, Jon also found time for indoor pursuits. From ages nine to eleven, he played the trumpet in the Lawrence Stage Band, a children's swing band. He made his first TV appearance as a member of that band when it was invited to play on a local Philadelphia children's show called *Captain Noah and His Magical Ark*. When asked in a 2002 interview about his TV debut, he said, "I performed poorly but I was part of a novelty act. All I can say is that Captain Noah was a mean man, who craved a smoke. Those are my memories of breaking into showbiz."[9]

A Broken Family

Jon's life changed when he was nine years old and his father left the family. His parents were divorced shortly thereafter. Donald Leibowitz went on to have two more sons with a new wife and made little attempt to stay in contact with Larry and Jon. His father's abandonment hurt Jon. When asked in a 1999 interview

Like Mother, Like Son

It is not surprising that both Jon Stewart and his brother, Larry, did well in school. They were raised by a well-respected educational consultant. Marian Leibowitz has a background working with gifted and talented children and has spent most of her career helping teachers be more effective. She continues to travel to schools, both in the New York area and across the country, to give presentations to teachers, parents, and administrators.

Leibowitz's youngest son may have gotten at least some of his ability to entertain from his mother. "She was witty, personal, motivational and truly entertaining," wrote two reporters who attended one of Leibowitz's lectures in 2010. "The apple clearly didn't fall far from the tree."

Stefani Cardone and Donna Hickman. "Marian Leibowitz Comes to South Riding." *Loudon Times*, October, 13, 2010. www.loudountimes.com/index.php/communities/article/marian_leibowitz_comes_to_south_riding.

what he learned from his father, he sarcastically replied, "If you don't get it right with your first family, you can always do it again with another. He's a very scientific man, and we were the control group."[10] He has also hinted that his father's abandonment is part of the reason why he ultimately discarded his last name.

Despite his parent's divorce, Jon continued to enjoy a fairly stable and normal childhood. Like many other Jewish children, Jon attended Hebrew school in order to prepare for his bar mitzvah. A bar mitzvah is a special coming-of-age ceremony for a Jewish boy when he is thirteen years old (girls have bat mitzvahs). During his bar mitzvah, a boy participates in a service by chanting long passages of Hebrew from a religious text called the Torah. A boy who has had a bar mitzvah is considered an adult in the Jewish religion. After the ceremony, there is a festive reception with plenty of food and gifts to honor the young man.

The reception for Jon's older brother's bar mitzvah was held in a fancy hotel. Unfortunately, by the time Jon turned thirteen, things had changed for his family, and they could no longer afford the hotel. Instead, Jon's bar mitzvah was held at the Princeton Jewish Center.

First Job Failures

Like many students, Jon worked part-time while he attended high school, or at least he tried to. Unlike his older brother, who was an excellent student and a responsible employee, Jon could

Stewart takes to the softball field as part of MTV's Rock 'n Jock event in 1992. As a teenager, Stewart was a good athlete, excelling at soccer.

not seem to hold a job. He was fired from six different jobs at the Quaker Bridge Mall near his home. The first was a bakery. It was his job to clean all of the machines. "I lined the dough mixer with soap and then forgot to actually wash it. The bakers came in the next morning, thought the soap was flour and made a batch of bread,"[11] he says.

As bad as that was, Jon's previous job struggles pale in comparison to the time he got fired from his job as a stock boy at Woolworth's, a now-defunct variety store. Jon tried to make his coworkers laugh by diving headfirst into a pile of beanbag chairs. Unfortunately, both he and the beanbags skidded into a wall of aquariums. The stunt destroyed ten thousand dollars' worth of aquarium equipment and killed hundreds of fish. "I was in the process of throwing the dead fish into the incinerator when the manager caught me and fired me," he recalls. "Then I had to go eat dinner with him because he was also my brother."[12]

Although he was not a good employee, Jon was a good student. He attended Lawrence High School from 1976 to 1980, and friends say he got good grades without trying too hard. Jon excelled at athletics as well and played on the school's varsity soccer team.

A Young Politico with a Sense of Humor

Jon's interest in politics also began in high school. In the late 1970s Republican Ronald Reagan was campaigning for president, and Jon was opposed to the conservative movement that supported Reagan. Despite his dislike of the future president, Jon was given the challenging assignment of portraying Reagan in a mock debate. He remembers being forced to defend positions he was opposed to, such as increased military spending. Jon's political beliefs were more liberal. He describes his political views when he was in high school as "very into [union leader] Eugene Debs and a bit of a leftist."[13]

While Jon took politics seriously, he was not always serious. He was not exactly a class clown, but both teachers and students

A campaign button promotes Republican presidential candidate Ronald Reagan in 1980. Stewart had to portray Reagan in a mock debate in high school.

took note of his sense of humor. "He was very funny, not funny in the sense that he would tell funny stories, more quick, witty," says Larry Nichol, Jon's twelfth-grade English teacher. "He'd always be saying something on the way out the door as the bell was ringing."[14] In 1980 Jon graduated from high school third in his class. In his yearbook his classmates voted him the graduate with the best sense of humor.

Soccer Dreams

Stewart attended the College of William & Mary in Williamsburg, Virginia. Stewart chose the small, conservative school because he was drawn to their soccer program. William & Mary had one of the best soccer programs in the nation, and at that time Stewart thought he might be able to play professionally someday. Although he was small, Stewart had been one of the best players on his high school team. However, the competition was tougher at William & Mary, and Stewart was both surprised and disappointed when he was placed on the junior varsity team at the start of his freshman year. He worked hard and was moved up to the varsity team in his sophomore year, where he played wing. "Jon was very feisty as a player, very high-energy sort of guy," says Al Albert, the coach at the time. "He played out wide. He worked very hard."[15] In addition to playing for his college team, Stewart was also an assistant coach for the Gloucester High School boys' soccer team in Gloucester, Virginia.

In 1983 Stewart was recruited to play on the U.S. team at the Pan American Maccabi Games in São Paulo, Brazil. The Maccabi Games are an Olympic-style event for Jewish athletes. They take place every four years. During the ten-day trip, Stewart attended dinners, parties, and Latin American as well as Jewish cultural events. "He created a little bit of levity," says David Coonin, one of Stewart's Maccabi teammates, "but everybody was always a little afraid of messing with Jon because he was so quick-witted."[16] Stewart was quick on the field as well. His team came in second place and lost to Brazil in the finals.

Although Stewart was a good player, his hopes of playing soccer professionally were dashed when he injured his knee toward the end of college. Despite his injury, Stewart was glad that he had the opportunity to play for William & Mary, and he even learned a valuable life lesson from the experience. "I had a great deal of pride in working my way onto the team and becoming a starter," Stewart says. "It gave me the confidence that there was a correlation between working hard and success and results and getting better at something."[17] Stewart's contribution to the team has not been forgotten. His hard work and his ability to make his teammates laugh are now honored by an award called the Leibo. Since 2006 this award has been given each year to the William & Mary soccer player who most demonstrates good humor and hard work.

Trying to Find His Place

From the outside, Stewart seemed to have the ideal college experience. He made friends, traveled with the soccer team, got good grades, and according to his roommate, was popular on campus. However, Stewart never really felt like he fit in on

The Wren Building is a landmark on the campus of the College of William & Mary, which Stewart attended. He also played on the school's soccer team.

the conservative Southern campus. "I went to college, I was 17, I didn't know anything," he says. "And [William & Mary] is a conservative place, coming from where I come from. ... And I did have a sense down there of not fitting in."[18]

One of the ways Stewart attempted to fit in was by joining a fraternity. Stewart was briefly a member of the Pi Kappa Alpha fraternity but dropped out because he felt that the friendships within the fraternity were not genuine. "It wasn't worth the pressure of living up to someone else's expectations of what you're supposed to be,"[19] he remembers. He eventually moved out of the fraternity and into a house with some of his soccer teammates.

Historic William & Mary

Chartered in 1693 by King William III and Queen Mary II while Virginia was still under British rule, William & Mary is the second-oldest college in the nation. Construction of the first building, the Sir Christopher Wren Building, began in 1695. Although it has burned down on three separate occasions, it was always rebuilt within the original walls, making it the oldest college building in the United States. The colonial town of Williamsburg was built around the college.

Stewart gives the commencement address at his alma mater, the College of William & Mary, in 2004.

William & Mary boasts many prestigious alumni. Three U.S. presidents—Thomas Jefferson, James Monroe, and John Tyler—graduated from the school. Twenty years after he graduated, Stewart was awarded an honorary doctorate degree from the university and gave the 2004 commencement address. In it he joked, "As a person, I am honored to get it; as an alumnus, I have to say I believe we can do better."

Jon Stewart. "Jon Stewart's ('84) Commencement Address." *William & Mary News*, May 20, 2004. http://web.wm.edu/news/archive/index.php?id=3650.

Stewart planned to become a veterinarian and originally majored in chemistry. He ended up switching to psychology, however, because he found humanities to be a better fit for his personality than the sciences. "Apparently there's a right and wrong answer in chemistry; whereas in psychology, you can say whatever you want as long as you write five pages,"[20] he once joked. Although he enjoyed some aspects of his major, he knew long before he graduated that he would not go into the field of psychology.

"When I left William and Mary I was shell-shocked,"[21] says Stewart, who graduated in 1984. Like many college graduates, Stewart felt lost and had no clear idea what he wanted do with his life. He returned to Trenton and for the next two years held a variety of odd jobs. At one point he had a job putting on puppet shows in elementary schools to help children learn how to be sensitive to disabled people. He also took a job with the New Jersey Department of Health that involved catching and sorting mosquitoes that were then tested for the disease encephalitis.

Stewart's Greatest Decision

It was while working as a state contingency planner that Stewart realized he might spend his whole life working at a job he did not really want. "I had my midlife crisis early," he says. "In 1986, I was living in Hamilton, New Jersey, working for the state and bartending and playing on a landscape company's softball team. I started thinking, 'This is it for the next seventy years?'"[22] It was then that he made the decision that would change his life: He decided to move to New York to pursue a career as a stand-up comedian. Years later, even after getting his own television show, Stewart still considered this moment to be his greatest achievement. He recalls:

> You know, somebody asked me the other day—they said, "Do you feel like you've done anything great?" I said, "No." And then I thought, "No, I have," and the one thing I did that was great was I moved from Trenton, New Jersey to New York, to try and become a comedian. That's the one thing I've done in this business that's great. Because I gave myself the opportunity to express whatever it was that I thought I needed to express.[23]

Stewart had little money and very little experience or knowledge about show business. But he also knew he had nothing to lose. He quit his job, sold his car, and headed for New York, making a leap from which he never looked back.

Chapter 2

Chasing the Dream

In the spring of 1986 Jon Stewart moved from Trenton to New York to start his new life as a comedian. The move took his family by surprise. "All Jon had ever done was host the high-school talent show," says his mother. "I didn't say it, but I figured, New York City is an hour and a half away, he'll be back soon enough."[24] Despite her doubts, Stewart's mother was supportive of the move. Stewart did not know if his father had an opinion on the move or his new career; by this time Stewart was so estranged from him that the two were not even speaking.

In New York Stewart took a job driving a van for a catering company. Although he spent much of his free time watching comedians at New York comedy clubs, it took Stewart nearly a year to work up the nerve to perform himself.

A Brutal Beginning

Stewart was twenty-four years old when he finally appeared onstage for the first time. In April 1987 he appeared at the Bitter End, a club in Greenwich Village. He chose the Bitter End for his first performance because it was where two of his favorite comedians—Woody Allen and Steve Martin—got their starts. Unlike Allen and Martin, however, Stewart's debut did not go well.

Stewart's timing was poor: he went on very late, at 1:00 A.M., and followed a rock band. While introducing him, the emcee mispronounced his last name, which was still Leibowitz. "I had about 4½ minutes of material prepared and was only about two

Stewart performs his stand-up routine in 2003. His career in comedy began in 1987 when he started playing clubs in New York City.

minutes into it when somebody in the audience called me a name," says Stewart. "It was absolutely brutal. I didn't finish the show and I didn't get back on a stage for a long time."[25]

Even though his act was a public failure, it was, to Stewart, a personal success. "It was a terrible night, but I knew what I wanted to do with the rest of my life. Just getting onstage made me realize that this is what has been going on in my head the last 20 years," says Stewart. "Knowing that, it wasn't hard to go back on a stage."[26]

Stewart next appeared during a weekly open mike night at the Comedy Cellar, another New York club. According to club owner Bill Grundfest, Stewart's act had not improved. Grundfest recalls, "He was getting nothing. He was bombing. He was dying a horrible, horrible death."[27] Despite Stewart's poor performance,

From Leibowitz to Stewart

Jon Stuart Leibowitz changed his stage name to Jon Stewart in 1987, the day after his first Bitter End performance at which the emcee mispronounced his last name. In addition to the emcee's mistake, Stewart had some lingering resentment about being teased for his last name as a child. Also, Stewart was still angry with his father for leaving the family and no longer wanted to use his name. Since then, he has joked that Leibowitz was "too Hollywood," which is part self-deprecating joke and part reference to Lenny Bruce, an influential Jewish-American comedian who also changed his name and, like Stewart, also focused much of his comedy around politics and current events. When Stewart and his wife were married, they both filed paperwork to change their legal last names to Stewart.

Quoted in Susan Howard. "Nighttime Talk, MTV Style." *Bergen County (NJ) Record,* 1994. http://jon.happyjoyfun.net/tran/1990/94_0000record.html.

Grundfest saw potential. He noted that Stewart seemed unafraid and unselfconscious, and he did not seem to dislike his audience, even though they clearly did not like him. Grundfest asked him back. Stewart got better, and eventually Grundfest hired him to emcee the late night show on Sunday through Thursday nights. For the next two years, Stewart honed his comedy skills at the Comedy Cellar and other clubs, earning himself a solid reputation as stand-up comedian.

From the Stage to the Small Screen

In 1988 Stewart was hired to open for pop singer Sheena Easton in Las Vegas. His act caught the attention of A&E Network executives, who invited him to write for a show called *Caroline's Comedy Hour* in 1989. Two years later a newly formed network called Comedy Central hired Stewart to cohost the show *Short*

Attention Span Theater with comic Patty Rosborough. The show featured entertainment news, occasional celebrity guests, and movie clips with commentary from the hosts. Rosborough remembers that Stewart often did not follow the rules on the show: "We would have this copy that the writers would write for us. And it was supposed to be funny, but it wasn't really funny, and Jon was like, 'I'm not reading this,' and I'm like, 'Really? Well what are we gonna do?' And he'd take it [the copy] and he'd just throw it in the garbage. He says, 'Okay let's just talk about something that happened today.'"[28]

Stewart left *Short Attention Span Theater* after a year to host a show on MTV called *You Wrote It, You Watch It*. In this show, viewers sent in sketches to be acted out by a troupe of comedians called "The State." Stewart's job was to introduce the sketches. This show only lasted for one season before it was cut in 1992 because of low ratings.

The Jon Stewart Show

Opportunity knocked for Stewart soon after, though, when he was offered his own talk show on MTV. *The Jon Stewart Show* was different than the well-financed talk shows on the major networks. The set was low budget. It featured an old van seat where guests sat and an air hockey table for the desk. Rather than the traditional suit and tie donned by most talk show hosts, Stewart wore jeans and a T-shirt. "We're a smaller show, just trying to keep it very playful and very fast-paced, trying to do the most fun show we can do,"[29] Stewart said at the time.

The show gained popularity quickly, becoming the second-highest rated show on the network. In 1994 Paramount Pictures tried to capitalize on the show's success by syndicating it for a wider audience. The show was expanded from half an hour to an hour and was shown across the nation on network TV. The new *Jon Stewart Show* received mixed reviews. Some critics felt that Stewart's casual approach was not right for network TV. Others appreciated the change and regarded Stewart's weaknesses as assets. For example, Ken Tucker of *Entertainment Weekly*

Stewart relaxes after the taping of the last episode of **The Jon Stewart Show** *in 1995. The show began on MTV and was soon syndicated to network television, but its ratings were poor.*

observed, "By network standards, Stewart is a far worse host, far less organized and polished—and that makes him more interesting to watch. He's more apt to say—or inspire his guests to say—something unexpected."[30]

Despite its popularity with the younger generation and its initial success on MTV, the syndicated, longer version of *The Jon Stewart Show* that aired to a broader audience did not get the ratings needed to stay on network TV. It was canceled in June 1995. "It's hard not to take it as a personal rejection," said Stewart at the time. "I was looking for a hug, and America spit in my face."[31]

Real Life Romantic Comedy

In addition to hosting TV, Stewart also pursued a movie career. Between 1994 and 1999, Stewart appeared in several mostly unsuccessful movies in small, silly parts. For example, in the 1994 film *Mixed Nuts*, he played a man on Rollerblade inline

Stewart appeared on the big screen in **The Faculty,** *one of several movies in which he was cast in the 1990s.*

skates with only one line. In the 1996 movie *The First Wives Club*, his part was so small it was cut from the final version of the movie. In *Half Baked*, a 1998 cult film starring actor and comedian Dave Chappelle, Stewart played a character known as "Enhancement Smoker." That same year he also played an alien-infested biology teacher who got his eye poked out with a pen in *The Faculty*.

In 1996 Stewart landed a part in *Wishful Thinking*, a romantic comedy starring Drew Barrymore that did so poorly in early screenings that it was released directly to video. Although the movie did not improve his career, it definitely changed Stewart's life. One of the women who worked as a production assistant on the set had a roommate named Tracey McShane, and the crew member thought Stewart would really enjoy meeting her. Stewart called McShane, and the two went on a blind date to a Mexican restaurant.

The date was actually only blind on Stewart's end. McShane, a veterinary technician, had not only seen Stewart on *The Jon Stewart Show*, but had even told her roommate she wanted to meet someone "funny and sweet like Jon Stewart."[32] Despite their eagerness to meet one another, the first date did not go well. Stewart was nervous and babbled through most of the meal; he thought McShane, who did not say much of anything, did not like him. Actually, McShane was merely embarrassed over how they met. As the evening progressed, McShane got over some of her own nervousness and talked more. Other dates followed, and before long the two were a couple.

Success as a First-Time Author

While Stewart was romancing McShane, he was also working on his first book, *Naked Pictures of Famous People*. Released in 1998, it is a collection of eighteen humorous essays that poke fun at celebrities, politics, and popular culture. Many of the essays are

His Own Production Company

In the mid-1990s, when Jon Stewart was the host of *The Jon Stewart Show*, he started Busboy Productions. Stewart named his production company after his experiences as a busboy before becoming a successful comedian.

Busboy Productions became very active after Stewart joined *The Daily Show*. Notable projects include *The Colbert Report*, hosted by former *Daily Show* correspondent Stephen Colbert, and stand-up comedian Demetri Martin's sketch comedy show, *Important Things with Demetri Martin*. Busboy Productions also produced the Stewart/Colbert Rally to Restore Sanity and/or Fear that was held in Washington, D.C., in November 2010.

Comedy Central provides the financial support for Busboy Productions and has a "first look agreement" for all of its projects. The agreement lets Comedy Central see Busboy's ideas and projects before other networks.

written not as if Jon Stewart were the author, but from the perspective of a particularly well-known person from either history or current events. Others are written from Stewart's point of view, but as if he got to meet or spend close personal time with famous people or their families. For example, in an essay called "Pen Pals," Princess Diana writes letters to an unresponsive Mother Teresa, telling her about her divorce from Prince Charles as if the two women are best friends:

Hey Girlfriend,

I know it's been a week since my last letter but things have been crazy here. Miss me? Anyway I'll get right to the point. Free at last, free at last. Thank God Almighty. … Free at last!!! The divorce came through days ago and I couldn't be more pleased. …

How are you? How's that thing going in India? Any new men? You're so pretty but you always play it down. I wish you'd let me make you over as I requested in my letters of May 12, 1994, August 5, 1995, and March 22, 1995.[33]

One of the last essays is written as a mock transcript of an interview Larry King might have had with Nazi leader Adolf Hitler. In it Hitler has resurfaced and, after a great deal of therapy, is ready to take responsibility for his role in World War II and the Holocaust. Rather than invading countries and killing people, the ex-führer has taken up word games, ballroom dancing, and the French horn. When asked about his behavior during the war, the newly enlightened Hitler replies, "Guilty as charged, Larry. Look, I was a bad guy, no question. *I* hate that Hitler. The yelling, the finger pointing, I don't know … I was a very angry guy."[34] Hitler then reveals that his rise to power was more about impressing women than world domination.

The book became a best seller and was generally well received by critics. Several noted that rather than just putting his monologues into writing as many other comedian authors did, Stewart wrote original pieces with a unique bent. He was praised for his wit, irreverence, and ability to poke fun at sensitive subjects such as the Holocaust. His style was compared favorably to that of comic icon Woody Allen, who wrote a trilogy of essays in the 1970s and 1980s. However, not everyone was impressed. Although he liked the Larry King interview with Adolf Hitler, book critic Tom Faucett wrote, "With a few rare exceptions, the essays are underdeveloped and flimsy, while some are simply muddled and incoherent. Cutting the number of essays in half, and really developing them, would have resulted in a much stronger offering."[35]

A Long Road to Talk Shows

Although Stewart's book was successful, his movie career was not, and he focused much of his energies during the late 1990s on furthering his presence as a television personality. He appeared as a guest on other shows, including the sitcoms *News Radio*, *The Nanny*, and *Spin City*. In 1996 he also hosted an HBO stand-up comedy special called *Jon Stewart: Unleavened*. Stewart was a regular guest on *The Larry Sanders Show*, an HBO sitcom about a talk show, which was hosted by and starred real-life comedian Gary Shandling. Celebrity guests appeared on the show, usually playing themselves, in a parody of the world of comedians and talk shows. Between 1996 and 1998, Stewart appeared nine times on *The Larry Sanders Show*.

Stewart also appeared on real talk shows. He chatted several times with David Letterman. He was also a frequent guest host on *The Late Late Show with Tom Snyder*, which was produced by Letterman and followed his show. In 1996 Stewart signed with Letterman's production company, *Worldwide Pants*, and most people assumed that he would eventually take over the show when Snyder retired.

In a move that puzzled critics and fans alike, however, Stewart was passed over for *The Late Late Show*. The slot was instead given to Craig Kilborn, the former sports commentator and host of a satirical news show called *The Daily Show* on Comedy Central. What seemed like a disappointment at the time, however, proved to be a career-defining moment for Stewart: When Kilborn left *The Daily Show* in 1999 to take over *The Late Late Show*, Stewart stepped in to take his place.

A Puzzling Proposal

Much to the delight of the four hosts of the talk show *The View*, Jon Stewart publicly announced his engagement to long-term girlfriend Tracey McShane during a guest appearance on June 30, 1999. Stewart proposed to McShane in a most unusual manner. He and McShane enjoyed doing the *New York Times* crossword puzzle together each night, so Stewart commissioned *Times* crossword editor Will Shortz to create a special puzzle just for McShane that included Stewart's proposal. As Stewart watched McShane solve the puzzle, he got a little worried. According to Stewart, McShane did poorly on the puzzle, even writing in the wrong name at one point. In the end, however, she solved the puzzle, and the two were married in 2000.

Stewart and his wife, Tracey, were married in 2000.

The Daily Show with Jon Stewart

Stewart was hired not only as the host but also as head writer and executive producer. The name of the show was changed from *The Daily Show* to *The Daily Show with Jon Stewart*. He was also offered $1.5 million dollars per year for his four-year contract, a

Stewart took over as host of Comedy Central's The Daily Show *in 1999 after Craig Kilborn left the program. The show was the cable network's second-highest rated show at the time.*

large amount for a cable station. "The overall budget of Comedy Central has now been drastically reduced," joked Madeleine Smithberg, cocreator and executive producer of *The Daily Show.* "Chef from *South Park* will have to go on a diet."[36]

Comedy Central had more than money to lose. In 1998 *The Daily Show* was its second-highest rated show, just behind *South Park.* Kilborn had been a popular host. Stewart had big shoes to fill, literally as well as figuratively. At well over 6 feet 4 inches tall (193cm), Kilborn is significantly taller than Stewart, who stands at 5 foot 7 inches (170cm). Stewart joked about his own size, saying, "They're getting rid of the tallest people on the show so that I don't look ridiculous."[37] As a joke, Kilborn left a phone book for Stewart on the host's chair. Kilborn hosted his last *Daily*

Show on December 17, 1998. After a few weeks of reruns, Stewart opened 1999 with his first show on January 11.

The Daily Show underwent many changes with Stewart as the host. Under Kilborn the show had focused on celebrities and pop culture. Stewart shifted the show's focus to news and politics. The show's tone also changed. Kilborn was known for his mean-spirited humor. He typically got laughs by making cruel jokes about celebrities or by making fun of people with extreme viewpoints, eccentric hobbies, or who appeared unintelligent on TV. This tone was adopted by the show's correspondents, who were frequently sent to interview people for the sole purpose of making them look idiotic. Occasionally interviewees were in on the joke and willing to play along, but more often they were not. "You wanted to take your soul off, put it on a wire hanger, and leave it in the closet before you got on the plane to do one of these pieces,"[38] says former correspondent Stephen Colbert.

By contrast, Stewart took a kinder approach. His likable persona and self-depreciating humor were a welcome, gentle change in the show's tone. Rather than picking on the underdog, he got laughs by making clever observations about the absurd actions and policies of government officials, corporate executives, and other powerful people. He got people to pay attention to news by pointing out the humor in it rather than mocking ordinary people. As Peter Keepnews of the *New York Times* puts it, "Mr. Stewart delivers the news with more of a conspiratorial wink than a condescending smirk."[39]

Stewart also wanted his correspondents to have their own perspectives, ideas, and values reflected in their segments and jokes. In doing so, he made political satire interesting to comedians who previously did not consider it part of their act. One of *The Daily Show*'s most successful correspondents is Stephen Colbert, who is now the host of his own politically themed comedy show and a best-selling author. Colbert remembers that he did not base his early act or jokes on politics. "I was never interested in political comedy." Colbert says. "Jon taught me how to do it so it would be smart. He encouraged everyone to have a point of view. There had to be a thought behind every joke."[40]

From Pop Culture to Politics

In the early days of the show, stories often focused on human-interest stories rather than hard news. For example, on May 25, 1999, the lead story was about Sherpa musicians from Nepal who played a concert on top of one of the World Trade Center buildings in order to perform the world's highest rock concert. Stewart joked, "The concert was staged for a new VH1 program called *Rock and Roll Record Breakers* as well as to celebrate VH1 being officially out of ideas."[41]

As the months passed, however, both Stewart and his correspondents took on harder news stories, but always with a humorous twist. The scandal-ridden presidency of Bill Clinton gave them plenty of material, as did the 2000 presidential election. On December 16, 1999, field correspondent Steve Carell did an *Indecision 2000* report that is widely regarded as a turning point for *The Daily Show*. Carell managed to get aboard presidential candidate Senator John McCain's campaign bus, *The Straight Talk Express*, by appealing to his wife. Just getting on the bus was a huge victory for the fake news show. Amazingly, Carell was offered an interview with the senator.

During the interview, Carell asked McCain a series of easy and silly questions, such as what his favorite movie was and if he were a tree, which one would he be. Then without changing his expression or tone, Carell suddenly asked: "How do you reconcile the fact that you were one of the most vocal critics of pork barrel politics, yet while you were chairman of the Commerce Committee, that committee set a record for unauthorized appropriations?" Taken completely off guard, McCain just stared back at him. A long moment passed before Carell started to laugh, saying, "I'm just kidding, I don't even know what that means!"[42]

It was a turning point for *The Daily Show* because Carell had managed to gain access to a real, high-profile presidential candidate. McCain was a powerful mainstream politician, a far cry from one of the eccentrics or oddballs more typically the subject of correspondent reports. Writer and executive producer Ben Karlin explains how that moment was a perfect example of a style *The Daily Show* has continued to develop and perfect.

*With **Stewart** as host, **The Daily Show** began shifting from its original pop-culture focus to cover political and social issues, making it more popular than ever.*

"That's a true fact, that question," he says, "and McCain was caught in the headlights. But we punctured it with a joke, so all you're left with is funny and awkward. It's bittersweet."[43] By the end of its first year with Jon Stewart, *The Daily Show* was even more popular than it had been when Kilborn hosted—and was about to receive even bigger accolades.

Chapter 3

The Daily Show Grows Up

Can a fake news show win a real award for journalism? In 2000 Jon Stewart and *The Daily Show* staff answered that question when they won their first of two George Foster Peabody Awards for excellence in radio and television broadcasting. This was a milestone for Stewart, *The Daily Show*, and Comedy Central, because the Peabody Awards are typically associated with journalism, documentary filmmaking, and educational programming. Winning the Peabody Award was a sign that Jon Stewart had embarked on a new kind of entertainment, one that was as serious and critical as it was hilarious.

Indecision Wins

Stewart's transition from little-known late-night comedian to Peabody Award winner was marked by his show's coverage of the 2000 presidential election. Stewart focused *The Daily Show* team around a special series of episodes and segments titled *The Daily Show: Indecision 2000*.

Indecision 2000 featured coverage of the presidential primaries in various states, interviews, and segments produced both in the New York City studios as well as on location at political events. *Daily Show* "correspondents" interviewed candidates, voters, and members of the media in an ongoing satire that portrayed the political process as more theatrical than substantive. Through satirical bits and insightful yet mocking pieces, they also cast the mainstream media as an echo chamber that offered little of journalistic value.

Indecision 2000 covered the run-up to the election, but it ended up as an appropriate name for the election itself. Due to voting irregularities in the state of Florida, the presidential race between Al Gore and George W. Bush remained undecided for weeks after election day. As the state of Florida engaged in multiple vote recounts and the candidates formed legal teams to challenge the process, Stewart noted how accurate his spoof had become. "Calling this whole thing Indecision 2000 was at first a bit of a light-hearted jab, perhaps an attempt at humor," he said. "We had no idea the people were going to run with that. We thought we were kidding, quite frankly. But Indecision is exactly where we are right now."[44]

When the 2000 election turned into a court battle between George W. Bush and Al Gore, Stewart and *The Daily Show* went from merely mocking the situation to skewering it. In particular they criticized the major news shows for their partisan coverage of the situation and presented reality as absurd theater in its own right. For example, prior to the night of the 2000 election, *Daily Show* correspondents found comedy in interviews with low-profile presidential impersonators and retained a playful tone with the candidates. Following election night, however, Stewart sharpened his satirical focus. Stewart remembers this as being a defining period for both him and the show. As he explains, "The 2000 recount was where we suddenly began to feel like we were connecting with everything we could do. That's when I think we tapped into the emotional angle of the news for us and found our editorial footing."[45]

The members of the Peabody Board clearly agreed. In their statement announcing the award for Jon Stewart and *The Daily Show*, they wrote: "Out of the convoluted sameness of media coverage of the last presidential election sprang the irreverent and inventive 'Daily Show with Jon Stewart: Indecision 2000.' Offering biting political satire, these scintillating segments had something droll and amusing to say about almost everything and

Stewart poses with the Peabody Award that his show won for its coverage of the 2004 presidential election. The show also won the award in 2000.

Comedy Central's Ongoing *Indecision*

Comedy Central had used the title *Indecision* once before for politically themed broadcasting, when Al Franken hosted the network's coverage of Bill Clinton's 1992 run to the White House. However, Jon Stewart developed the concept further. Under Stewart's lead, *Indecision* satirizes more than just politics—it also takes aim at how the news media covers politics. Stewart has continued to use the *Indecision* title and concept to cover numerous American and international elections. In addition, Stephen Colbert, host of *The Colbert Report* on Comedy Central and former *Daily Show* correspondent, has also used the *Indecision* title to frame his show's coverage of elections.

Stephen Colbert, left, and Stewart host Comedy Central's election coverage show, Indecision 2008: America's Choice.

everyone associated with American politics and the presidential election."[46]

In 2004 *The Daily Show with Jon Stewart* won a second Peabody Award for the production of *Indecision 2004*, the segment about that year's presidential election. The win helped legitimize both Stewart and his show. Although major news outlets such as CNN and National Public Radio won Peabody Awards for other types of programs and coverage of other topics, Jon Stewart and *The Daily Show* won the only Peabodies for presidential election coverage in both 2000 and 2004.

The September 11 Terrorist Attacks

By the summer of 2001 Stewart and his team of correspondents were working through a regular rotation of political news, current events, sports, entertainment and human-interest stories. In late August 2001 the staff went on vacation and was scheduled to return on September 10. In their first show back from vacation, Stewart and his team worked through some stories that were typical fare for the summer of 2001: an unusual lawsuit between a religious group and a publishing company, the role of sex in advertising, and then-president George W. Bush's perceived lack of a plan for rising unemployment. The next day changed the lives of countless Americans, Jon Stewart's life included.

On the morning of September 11, 2001, the world was shocked by the al Qaeda–led terrorist attacks against the United States. In a coordinated attack, terrorists hijacked and crashed passenger jets into both of the largest buildings in the World Trade Center in Manhattan as well as a third plane into one side of the Pentagon in Washington, D.C. A fourth plane was supposed to be part of the attacks, but passengers overwhelmed the terrorists and crashed in a field in rural Pennsylvania. Nearly three thousand people were killed in the combined attacks.

The United States and the world struggled to comprehend the attacks, which were the deadliest terrorist attacks in history. Because 9/11 took place on American soil, and because it brought a new global conflict into focus for many Americans, it was compared to the attack on Pearl Harbor, Hawaii, during World War II. In New York large portions of southern Manhattan were closed to the public; many businesses temporarily ceased work; New Yorkers roamed the streets in search of loved ones who were missing after the attacks.

"Any Fool Can Destroy"

The Daily Show returned to the air only nine days later, on September 20, 2001. From the first frame, the first show back was unlike any other. To begin with, the show did not run its usual introduction, which had featured a "fly-in" sequence that prominently showed the Twin Towers at the World Trade Center. Instead, the show simply opened with Jon Stewart sitting at his desk. Stewart embarked on a nine-minute monologue in which he tearfully reflected on what the terrorist attacks meant to him, as well as what he hoped they could mean for the entire nation. As a resident of New York City who lived in lower Manhattan near the World Trade Center, and worked at *The Daily Show* studios nearby, the attacks were especially personal to him.

"They said to get back to work," said a somber Stewart. "There were no jobs available for a man in the fetal position under his desk crying, which I gladly would have taken."[47] The audience, which had largely been quiet in the opening minutes of the show, broke into their first laugh at this line. Stewart struggled to hold back tears as he explained how much he values the freedom of expression found in American society, repeatedly referring to it as a privilege, especially in comparison to the "closed" societies that had attacked the United States.

He continued, sharing that one of his earliest memories was of the assassination of civil rights leader Martin Luther King Jr. in 1968, when Stewart was five years old. Although he could not understand that tragedy at the time, Stewart explained that in the recovery after 9/11, "we are judging people not by the color of their skin, but the content of their character." Stewart concluded by saying: "Any fool can blow something up. Any fool can destroy. But to see these guys, these firefighters, these policemen from all over the country, literally, with buckets, rebuilding. That's extraordinary. And that's why we've already won."[48]

Stewart concluded with the hopeful sentiment that the attacks could bring Americans together and inspire them to become an even greater beacon of prosperity and freedom for the world. He suggested that no terrorist could destroy the liberty that is at the essence of the United States. As he put it: "The view from my apartment was the World Trade Center, and now it's gone. They attacked it. This symbol of American ingenuity and strength and labor and imagination and commerce and now it's gone. But you know what the view is now? The Statue of Liberty. The view from the south of Manhattan is now the Statue of Liberty. You can't beat that."[49]

A Growing Process

If the 2000 presidential election and recounts had helped Stewart and his show begin to transition from a funny fake news show to one of relevant political satire and focused criticism, then the September 11 terrorist attacks helped him complete that process. Following 9/11, Stewart focused more on current events, such as President George W. Bush's handling of the subsequent wars in Afghanistan and Iraq as well as domestic political policies.

Before 9/11, *The Daily Show* guest list was similar to other late night talk shows: actors promoting movies, musicians promoting albums, authors promoting books. By 2002, however, the lineup began to change to reflect the show's shifting focus. While entertainers still visited *The Daily Show*, politicians, newscasters, political columnists, and other key players in current events increasingly populated the guest list. As the United States entered wars in both Afghanistan and Iraq and the 2004 election loomed on the horizon, Jon Stewart increasingly interviewed politicians such as Republican senator John McCain and Democratic representative Dennis Kucinich. In a first for Comedy Central—and for any comedy show, in fact—Democratic senator John Edwards officially announced

Democratic presidential candidate Senator John Kerry appears on The Daily Show *in 2004. By the mid-2000s, politicians and other prominent newsmakers were regular guests on Stewart's program.*

his candidacy for the 2004 presidential election on *The Daily Show*. The announcement helped underscore a reality that had been developing for several years: that *The Daily Show* was not just a place for laughs, but also for serious commentary and conversation.

Emerging Media Critic

In addition to focusing more heavily on politics and current events, Stewart began to increase focus on how such events are covered by the mainstream media. Partisan reporters, softball journalists, and sensational media outlets became a focus of criticism, satire, and even disgust for Stewart. Members of the media had previously been frequent targets of Stewart's comedy. As the Peabody Board noted when presenting its 2000 award to *The Daily Show*, "[Stewart lampoons] reporters for taking themselves too seriously."[50] By 2004, however, Stewart and his staff were routinely exposing bias and hypocrisy in major news shows and well-known media figures.

If Stewart were to have had a coming out party as a powerful media critic, it would have been held on October 15, 2004, when he was a guest on the CNN current issues program *Crossfire*, with Tucker Carlson and Paul Begala. Although he was supposed to appear on the show to promote a new book written by *Daily Show* staff, Stewart instead took aim at *Crossfire's* premise, claiming it was "hurting America."[51] At the time, *Crossfire* was typical of many cable news programs. It boiled political and social issues down to overly simplified arguments that fit neatly into a pro-con, and often misleading, Democrat vs. Republican or conservative vs. liberal framework. In his appearance Stewart cast himself as a representative of the people and criticized *Crossfire*

Paul Begala, left, and Tucker Carlson debate on CNN's Crossfire. Stewart's on-air criticism of the program's premise and its hosts' behavior led to its cancellation.

for intentionally misrepresenting the serious issues of the day to drum up ratings and further the interests of powerful politicians and major corporations.

Stewart argued that *Crossfire* was not a debate show, as the hosts claimed, but rather theater. He accused the hosts of being complicit in a media conspiracy that undermined the best interests of the American people. "You are part of their strategy. You are partisan, what do you call it, hacks," he said. When the hosts tried to claim that *Crossfire* was about debate, Stewart argued, "What you do is not honest" and said that characterizing *Crossfire* as debate was "like saying pro wrestling is a show about athletic competition."[52]

Crossfire cohost Tucker Carlson shot back that Stewart failed to live up to the high standards he set for others in the media. For example, Carlson attacked Stewart for the way he conducted a 2004 interview with Democratic presidential nominee John Kerry, claiming that Stewart's questions were too easy. Carlson said that Stewart had missed an opportunity to "ask a real question."[53] Stewart countered that he "did not realize, and maybe this explains quite a bit, that news organizations look to Comedy Central for cues on integrity."[54] Each time Carlson tried to engage Stewart on the quality of his interview with John Kerry, Stewart returned to the defense that as a comedian, he is not responsible for serious journalism.

The Shot Heard 'Round the Internet

The clip of Stewart's appearance on *Crossfire* was viewed by over 3 million people, although most saw it online after it aired. Stewart later joked, "It was definitely viral. I felt nauseous afterwards."[55]

Stewart's comments set off a storm of further comments, criticism, and columns in other media outlets. The *New York Times* praised Stewart for "[saying] what a lot of viewers feel helpless to correct: that news programs, particularly on cable, have become echo chambers for political attacks, amplifying the noise instead of parsing the misinformation."[56] Others

Jon Stewart, Author

Along with his initial success in 1998 with *Naked Pictures of Famous People,* Jon Stewart has coauthored two books with the writers of *The Daily Show.* Together, they wrote and published *America (The Book): A Citizen's Guide to Democracy Inaction* in 2004 and *Earth (The Book): A Visitor's Guide to the Human Race* in 2010.

America (The Book) is presented as a satire and parody of a typical American high school civics textbook. Although it is full of jokes, nonsensical whimsy, and obviously untrue information, it is written with enough of a historical base to be classified as a nonfiction book. It was named "Book of the Year" by *Publishers Weekly.*

Stewart poses with a copy of America (The Book), *which he coauthored with other writers of* The Daily Show *in 2004.*

Earth (The Book) is written as a travel guide for aliens visiting Earth at some undetermined date in the future. The book also acts as a brief history of the world, although it seems to assume that human civilization on this planet has gone extinct.

criticized his tendency to hide behind his identity as a comedian as a way of dodging responsibility. Dan Kennedy of the *Boston Phoenix* wrote:

> By offering serious media criticism, and then throwing up his hands and saying in effect, "Hey, I'm just a comedian" every time Carlson took him on, Stewart came off as slippery and

disingenuous [insincere]. Sorry, Jon, but you can't interview [former president] Bill Clinton, [former chief counterterrorism advisor] Richard Clarke, [Fox News commentator] Bill O'Reilly, [former senator] Bob Dole, etc., etc., and still say you're just a comedian.[57]

One important person who did agree with Stewart was Jonathan Klein, the new president of CNN. Within two months, Klein canceled *Crossfire* and fired Carlson, saying, "I agree wholeheartedly with Jon Stewart's overall premise."[58] Klein also said, "I think [Stewart] made a good point about the noise level of these types of shows, which does nothing to illuminate the issues of the day."[59]

Daily Show Viewers Grow Up, Too

By 2004 Stewart had attracted more than just heavy-hitting awards and critical media attention—he had attracted a savvy audience, too. In several surveys that measured the public's knowledge of current events, *Daily Show* viewers consistently ranked among the best informed in the nation.

The Program on International Policy Attitudes (PIPA) made waves in 2003 when it quizzed the public on three false claims about the U.S.-led war in Iraq. PIPA found that there is a relationship between people's knowledge of current events and their news source, regardless of other factors like education. Soon after this study, similar surveys began to include *The Daily Show with Jon Stewart* as a choice in their list of news sources. What they found suggested that *The Daily Show* and Jon Stewart were distributing more than just laughs; they might actually have been educating their viewers.

In 2004 the University of Pennsylvania's National Annenberg Election Survey found that "*Daily Show* viewers have higher campaign knowledge than national news viewers and newspaper readers—even when education, party identification, following politics, watching cable news, receiving campaign information online, age, and gender are taken into

A student watches Comedy Central's 2008 election coverage led by Stephen Colbert and Stewart while monitoring returns on his laptop. Surveys have shown that people who watch The Daily Show *tend to be well informed of current events.*

consideration."[60] A 2007 Pew Research Center survey similarly found *Daily Show* viewers to be more informed than audiences of news shows on Fox, CNN, or National Public Radio. The Pew Research Center determined that 54 percent of *Daily Show* viewers had a "high level of knowledge" about current events and political subjects—the highest score recorded. *Daily Show* viewers tied with readers of newspapers and were better informed than consumers of Internet news (who ranked between 41 and 44 percent), network evening news watchers (38 percent), blog readers (37 percent), Fox News Channel viewers (35 percent), local TV news watchers (35 percent), and audiences of morning news (34 percent).

"What's Up Nerds!"

The Daily Show audience's high level of knowledge did not necessarily mean the show was educating them, critics were quick to point out. The jokes presume a certain level of knowledge, and thus *The Daily Show* is likely to attract an audience that probably either is already interested in or already knows about such topics. Furthermore, *Daily Show* viewers were found to be more likely to be better educated and wealthier than viewers of other programs. For example, the 2004 Annenberg survey found that *Daily Show* viewers were 78 percent more likely than the average American to have four or more years of college education; viewers of Fox's *O'Reilly Factor*, by comparison, were only 24 percent more likely to have that level of education. This fact could also explain the higher level of knowledge among viewers of *The Daily Show*. As Dannagal Goldthwaite Young, an Annenberg Public Policy Center analyst, explains: "These findings do not show that *The Daily Show* is itself responsible for the higher knowledge among its viewers."[61]

Stewart addresses the audience at a taping of **The Daily Show**, *which has viewers that tend to be better educated and wealthier than those of other politically oriented programs.*

But the findings did put to rest accusations made by traditional journalists that viewers of comedy programs like *The Daily Show* receive poor or erroneous information or even fail to develop a taste for the news and important issues. "This data suggests that these fears may be unsubstantiated,"[62] says Young.

Stewart appeared satisfied that viewers of Fox News, one of his most frequent targets of ridicule, were typically the least informed. "Our viewers are actually better educated than [Fox News host Bill] O'Reilly's viewers and the University of Pennsylvania actually had a study saying that *Daily Show* viewers are more well versed in current events than people who only watch news channels," he said with surprise and pride on the show one night. But proving that he had not grown up too much, Stewart added: "I have to say this to our viewers: 'What's up nerds!'... We here at the show are clearly in way over our heads."[63]

Chapter 4

The Voice of the People

While Jon Stewart does not typically discuss his personal beliefs outright, he tends to be a champion of "the little guy," sticking up for people when he thinks they are exploited, oppressed, or otherwise wronged by corporations, politicians, or the mainstream media. In much of Stewart's commentary, he casts himself as a representative of regular Americans and presents politicians, corporations, and the mainstream media as colluding, or secretly cooperating, with each other at the little guy's expense.

The People's Media Watchdog

Stewart frequently targets the mainstream media for failing the American people on several levels. He often complains that media giants like Fox News, CNN, or CNBC create confusion and hysteria rather than informing people; that they misrepresent or sensationalize information to improve their ratings; and most of all, that they fail to hold corporations, politicians, and government accountable for taking advantage of or even committing crimes against the American people. Stewart's criticism of the media is typically delivered as a hybrid of edited video clips interspersed with his commentary. These parody the actions and statements of politicians or corporate leaders and slam the often-synchronized response of the traditional news media.

Stewart's media montages frequently expose the hypocrisy of news personalities by featuring them as ineffectual, silly, biased, or hypocritical. In one segment in 2011, for example, Stewart revealed layers of hypocrisy in Fox News's coverage of controversial cuts in teacher pay. He did this by contrasting it with Fox's coverage of taxes for America's best-paid individuals and reporting of pay for chief executive officers (CEOs) of banks, which was supported by tax dollars.

Stewart bounced back and forth between clips of Fox News personalities and inserted his own comedic analysis. First, he showed Fox News pundits claiming that teachers who earn $50,000 a year are overpaid—then Stewart showed them claiming that Americans who earn $250,000 a year are not rich and cannot afford slightly higher taxes. Next Stewart showed Fox News commentators arguing that state governments can and should cut public employees' pay—seconds later, he showed the same people arguing against limiting the pay of executives—even those who do a bad job—at banks that were being supported by public money. Stewart furthered the contrast by showing Fox News commentators argue that Wall Street executives were owed big bonuses because they had legal contracts. Seconds later, Stewart showed the exact same commentators argue that teachers should ignore their contracts and give up their pay or benefits. Stewart revealed that the commentators simply reversed their arguments, showing their bias in favor of bankers or the wealthy and their disdain for teachers and other public employees. This is an example of one of many segments in which Stewart pieces together clips to reveal hypocrisy and bias in the news media.

Another of Stewart's pet peeves is when media personalities—and politicians, for that matter—make extreme comparisons, such as likening American presidents or business leaders to Nazi leader Adolf Hitler. He believes this only serves to ramp up rhetoric (discourse or speech), divide the American people, and prevent them from understanding, discussing, and solving real issues and problems. So, when Fox News host Megyn Kelly denied claims that Fox News personalities frequently compare Americans to Nazis, Stewart was ready with a mother lode of clips showing nearly every star of Fox News—including the Fox News president Roger Ailes

Fox News host Megyn Kelly and other personalities on that network became a target of Stewart's criticism because of their practice of using extreme language, such as comparisons to Adolf Hitler, during their broadcasts.

and a previous guest on Kelly's show—using Nazi rhetoric, or language, to refer to those they disagree with. Seemingly whenever a politician or news commentator contradicts him- or herself, Jon Stewart and his *Daily Show* team have it on tape and ready to use.

Stewart has been both praised and criticized for this technique. Some view him as engaging in some of the highest-quality journalism around. The *Nation*, for example, praised Stewart for doing "yeoman [helpful] work for the rest of us by exposing the thoughtlessness of the punditocracy's perpetual-motion machine [nonstop media coverage], which spins itself silly powered only by hot air."[64] Similarly, the British newspaper the *Guardian* described him as "the last best hope in the media when it comes to, in the earnest phrase of news network CNN, 'keeping them honest.'" *Guardian* reporter David Smith went on to praise Stewart for acting as a lone watchdog when others in the news media failed to perform their critical function: "It was this comedian who, like a court jester, told uncomfortable truths about the Iraq war when the mainstream media was playing cheerleader. Now, as the financial apocalypse unfolds, it is Stewart again who is scything [cutting] through the herd mentality and culture of deference [putting another person's interests first—or in the case of CNBC, putting corporate interests or those of powerful investors first]."[65]

However, others have called Stewart's video montages selectively edited, inaccurate, and biased. "Stewart's staff obviously just did a [Lexis] Nexis or some other computer search on the word Nazi and those are the four hits that they got," wrote conservative columnist and author John Lott about *The Daily Show*'s attack on Megyn Kelly. "Stewart is simply dishonest and if his viewers don't pick up on how he changed the statements by Kelly through the course of the segment, they are not very smart."[66] Still others have called Stewart's belief that the news media exist to enlighten and empower the people naive and overly simplistic. "The media most certainly does not have a 'responsibility to the public discourse,'" argues journalist Michael Moynihan. He notes that Stewart seems obsessed with the idea of journalists reporting the truth, adding, "The comedian is obsessed with the question of why journalists couldn't find ways to report the 'truth.' But

Stewart has a lot to learn about the news if he thinks there is one 'truth' to be reported."[67] Despite such criticism, Stewart contends it is the mainstream media's job to be, as he puts it, "a powerful tool of illumination"[68] for American people, and he makes it a priority to hold the media accountable to that standard.

WGA Strike

Stewart again played the role of champion of the people against the powerful media, corporate, and political insider's world on November 5, 2007, when the Writers Guild of America (WGA) went on strike. Stewart, who is a vocal supporter of unions, had been instrumental in getting his show's writers unionized. In fact, *Daily Show* writers were the first writers on Comedy Central to join the union, which represents film, radio, and

Striking Writers Guild members picket the studios of The Daily Show in January 2008. Although the strike put his show off the air for several weeks and affected the content of his broadcasts, Stewart was vocal in his support for the writers.

television writers working across America. Through the WGA, writers can bargain as a group with their employers for better pay or health benefits.

By November 2007, however, the WGA had taken issue with several policies of its major employer, the Alliance of Motion Picture and Television Producers, a trade group that represents hundreds of studios and corporations that produce entertainment programming. For Stewart and the writers of *The Daily Show*, one major concern was that writers were being compensated with an outdated system for DVD sales of the show and had no uniform method for receiving payment for its online viewings. *The Daily Show* attracts thousands, even millions of online viewers, but WGA writers had no deal with any studio to be paid for Internet-based viewings or online programming. Therefore, the writers went on strike to negotiate for a better deal.

Without writers, the show was forced to shut down. *The Daily Show with Jon Stewart* went on hiatus, and Comedy Central aired reruns. Although Stewart is a member of the WGA and supported the writers' strike, in January 2008 he eventually went back to doing live shows without his writers. Stewart was concerned about the show's nonwriters, such as camera operators and sound technicians, who would be out of work as long as he was not producing new episodes. The WGA speculated that corporate executives had forced Stewart back on the air by threatening the jobs of writers and other crew members.

During this time he referred to the program as "*A Daily Show*" instead of "*The Daily Show.*" In place of segments that would ordinarily be written by WGA members, Stewart interacted with the hosts of other talk shows, such as Stephen Colbert and Conan O'Brien. O'Brien explained, "Shows like [ours] are hybrids with both written and non-written content. An unwritten version of Late Night, though not desirable, is possible—and no one has to be fired."[69] For his part, Stewart, laughed through obviously improvised sketches, abided by strict rules for what he could do on the air without violating the strike, and even played the sound of WGA members picketing his own show. He tried to walk a fine line between supporting the strikers and keeping the show on the air so that non-WGA workers who worked for

The Daily Show—like janitors and cameramen—could keep their jobs too. He successfully walked this line until the strike ended in February 2008.

Jon Stewart and the Financial Crisis

Stewart continued to play the role of champion of the people throughout 2008 and 2009, when the United States and much of the world was hit by a global financial crisis, in part brought on by the actions of major American banks. By the spring of 2009, the federal government was using trillions of dollars in taxpayer money to save some of the largest banks and Wall Street financial firms from collapse in a move that became known as the "bailout." Throughout this crisis, Stewart typically took the side of ordinary people, thousands of whom suddenly found themselves out of work or facing foreclosure on their homes.

Foreclosure signs became a common sight in neighborhoods throughout the United States during the recession in the late 2000s. Corporations, the media, and the government were frequent targets of criticism by Stewart for their role in the financial crisis.

The Global Financial Crisis

Jon Stewart has devoted many segments to the exploration of the global financial crisis that began in 2008. This was when America and much of the world was rocked by a financial catastrophe described by economists as the worst financial crisis since the Great Depression. The crisis caused major banks to fail, the U.S. stock market to crash, housing prices to plummet, and unemployment to skyrocket; it also triggered a major economic recession and led the U.S. federal government to step in and bail out formerly enormous and powerful sectors of the economy with trillions of dollars.

As the center of the financial industry in the United States, Wall Street in New York came to symbolize the cause of the global financial crisis of the late 2000s.

The root causes of the financial crisis center around complex financial products known as mortgage-backed securities. Previously viewed as a way for investors to make money on rising housing prices, mortgage-backed securities spawned an economy of their own with a variety of spin-off products that investors buy and sell in complex financial deals. However, the interconnected nature of these securities with homeowners' mortgages and a variety of banks and investments led to a domino effect of financial failures.

Some journalists have reported that financial insiders committed fraud for personal profit and that this led to the crisis. Because of suspected fraud and the perception that financial insiders got rich while ordinary Americans lost out, the causes of the financial crisis and resulting recession remain controversial.

In numerous episodes of *The Daily Show*, Stewart wryly commented on the layers of corporate greed and lack of media and government oversight that had contributed to the crisis. This commentary came to a head in early March 2009, when Stewart focused some of his most scathing criticism on the business news network CNBC.

Stewart took aim at CNBC after one of its analysts, Rick Santelli, engaged in a televised rant from the trading floor of the Chicago Mercantile Exchange, a type of marketplace in which various financial products are bought and sold. Backed by representatives of and investors in some of the same firms that had accepted the taxpayer-funded bailout money, Santelli called homeowners struggling in the recession "losers." Santelli also criticized a government proposal designed to help people keep their homes. While Santelli yelled into the camera, financial workers supported him in the background, showing their anger over the situation. Stewart was not amused, and he devoted over a week of shows to exposing the failings of CNBC.

On the first night, Stewart showed highlights of Santelli's rant and then yelled in mock indignation, "Yeah! Wall Street is mad as hell, and they're not going to take it anymore! Unless by 'it,' you mean $2 trillion in their own bailout money. That, they will take."[70] Stewart focused on the bailout money because it came from the general public's taxes. Taxpayer money was being used to "bail out," or save, the very financial institutions that had caused the financial crisis—the same crisis that now led many taxpayers to lose their jobs and homes. In Stewart's opinion, Santelli's attack on a government program designed to help ordinary citizens was deeply unjust and hypocritical.

From there, Stewart launched into a larger indictment of CNBC. He showed a montage of CNBC news anchors and media personalities repeatedly giving not just bad financial advice, but advice that played to the interests of banks and corporations rather than individual investors. In clip after clip, CNBC analysts were seen enthusiastically advising people to invest their money in firms that quickly failed, went bankrupt, or otherwise lost money. Some CNBC personalities advised viewers to put their money into large banks that then failed. Some allowed financial CEOs to promote their companies on the air. In one clip CNBC anchors even joked around with a man who was later charged with stealing billions of dollars from his investors. Stewart wryly joked, "If I'd only followed CNBC's advice, I'd have a million dollars today—provided I started with a hundred million dollars."[71] Through the clips and jokes, Stewart's point was unmistakable: CNBC had a track record not of financial journalism, but of promoting the financial industry, even as that industry collapsed the world economy.

Stewart was not finished, though. The next night, he appeared on *Late Night with David Letterman*, where he further criticized the financial news networks for poor journalism. CNBC's on-air personalities were watching and began to respond on their own shows. Stewart and his staff seemed to delight in the exchanges, and they continued to run clips that showed CNBC analysts offering bad or self-serving financial advice.

"I Can't Tell You How Angry It Makes Me"

One of the CNBC personalities most upset by the exchanges was Jim Cramer, host of the show *Mad Money*, which gives financial advice to prospective investors. Cramer appeared on another NBC show to complain about the attention from Stewart and *The Daily Show*. *The Daily Show* continued to mock him, and this proved to be too much for Cramer and CNBC.

On March 12 Cramer confronted Stewart on *The Daily Show*. For much of the interview, Stewart abandoned his identity as a comedian and took on the voice of people frustrated with what they saw as collusion between powerful corporations and the journalists tasked with covering them. The interview quickly took the tone of a courtroom prosecution. Stewart leveled two main charges: that CNBC failed to follow basic guidelines of journalism (which is to critically analyze the statements and actions of powerful newsmakers), and that CNBC promoted the financial markets that bankrupted ordinary investors while making executives and insiders rich in the process.

Jim Cramer, left, host of CNBC's Mad Money *program, squares off with Stewart during a broadcast of* The Daily Show *in March 2009. Stewart was a sharp critic of some of the financial advice that Cramer and other CNBC personalities gave to their viewers.*

Initially, Cramer tried to deflect Stewart's criticism. He apologized for making some "bad calls," but this opened the door for Stewart to levy his larger criticism: that insiders dominate the financial markets and manipulate the system for their profit while ordinary investors lose. Stewart said, "I think the difference is not good call, bad call. The difference is real market and unreal market." Stewart then aired video clips of Cramer explaining how he had manipulated financial markets, gotten around the law, and avoided government regulators to make money. The implication was clear: This was done at the expense of ordinary investors. Stewart drove his point home when he said, "I want the Jim Cramer that's on CNBC to protect me from that Jim Cramer," to audience applause. Cramer then sat in silence as Stewart said, "I know you want to make finance entertaining, but it's not a [expletive] game. When I watch that I can't tell you how angry it makes me, because what it says to me is, 'You all *know* [what you're doing is wrong].'"[72]

In Stewart They Trust

Cramer conceded the point that the business insiders employed by CNBC did not act effectively as journalists. In his defense he said that CEOs lied to him and that he made the mistake of overly trusting the businesspeople who had caused the financial collapse. However, Cramer tried to shrug off the fact that his show and others on CNBC made it seem easy to get rich through investing, because the shows attracted viewers. As he put it,

Media Criticism for the Internet Generation

Jon Stewart's relentless satire of powerful figures in the media and current events has earned him and *The Daily Show* the trust of a generation of viewers raised in a world of multimedia, digital video recorders, and the Internet. Indeed, part of Stewart's appeal is his reflection of the Internet generation's methods of accessing information. One of Stewart's signature comedic bits is to show the repeated use of a particular keyword or idea across multiple video clips to highlight hypocrisy or bias. In doing so, Stewart reflects how Internet users typically access information—they search for a keyword or idea and access a variety of media that feature the keyword.

"There's a market for it and you give it to them."[73] To which Stewart exclaimed, "There's a market for cocaine and hookers! So what?"[74]—the point being that just because there is a demand for something does not mean it is appropriate to provide it.

Stewart's preparation for the interview was apparent. Repeatedly, he commanded his crew off camera to show specific video clips, calling out, "roll two-ten," "roll two-twelve" or "now, two-sixteen!"[75] to access specific quotes for specific purposes. His explanations and insights into complex financial matters were clear and understandable. Most of all, the seriousness with which he approached the topic showed his belief that the economy had been seriously hurt by the greed of the financial industry and the incompetence of the mainstream media. Stewart appeared determined to get someone to take responsibility for their part in it.

Stewart's skewering of Cramer, CNBC, and others at fault in the financial crisis increased his popularity and contributed to his emerging identity as a "voice of the people." As David Folkenflik of National Public Radio put it, "Stewart crystallizes the frustration others have with the failings of the media with near-perfect pitch."[76] Mark A. Perigard of the *Boston Herald* agreed and praised Stewart for featuring "more trenchant [forceful] talk of the financial crisis and the responsibility of the networks than you'd find on any news channel, all the more surprising in that it aired on Comedy Central. It demonstrated once again why so many rely on Stewart for their news."[77] Eric Alterman of the *Nation* also had praise for the satirist. "Stewart, first by eviscerating [gutting] the coverage of CNBC and second by forcing Jim Cramer to own up to his on-air hucksterism, has revealed the lie at the center of most business coverage (and just about all cable news)."[78]

Speaking Out for Unions and Teachers

Another event in which Stewart stuck up for the little guy took place in 2011, when Republican governor Scott Walker of Wisconsin made headlines for proposing controversial limits to public employee unions as a way to resolve Wisconsin's budget

Teachers, state workers, and other protesters in Madison, Wisconsin, voice their opposition to Governor Scott Walker's budget cuts and anti-union policies in February 2011. Stewart came to the defense of teachers when some news personalities and politicians blamed the financial crisis on their labor deals.

deficit. The proposal, which sparked widespread protests in the state's capital in February 2011, prohibited state employee union members, such as teachers, firefighters, and police officers, from participating in collective bargaining, which is a key feature and purpose of union organizations that empowers a large group of employees to speak to their employer with one collective voice. Conservatives argued that unions used their numbers to gain extra benefits and compensation. Liberals argued that without banding together through collective bargaining and a union presence, many workers have no way to negotiate with their bosses.

The Daily Show responded to the incident by playing clips of pundits and politicians casting teachers as greedy, overpaid lazy people who abused their power to gain expensive benefits and squandered public tax dollars. *Daily Show* correspondent Samantha Bee parodied the MTV show *Cribs*, which takes viewers on a tour of outrageously plush celebrity mansions. Bee visited the modest homes of teachers, where she pretended to be amazed by "luxuries" like indoor plumbing and beds complete with "a top sheet *and* a bottom sheet."[79]

Stewart mocked news analysts and politicians who claimed that teacher salaries and benefits had significantly contributed to the financial crisis. He played video clips of Fox News analysts who argued against teachers but defended the distribution of extraordinarily high bonuses to Wall Street executives, despite their role in the crisis. Stewart took aim at the ridiculousness of characterizing teachers as greedy and lazy, saying satirically, "[Teachers] are destroying America. Yeah. Look at you, with your chalk-stained irregular blouses from Loehmans, and your Hyundai with its powered steering and its windshield. I guess bugs hitting you in the face doesn't cut it for old Mr. Chips. ... The greed that led you into the teaching profession has led to the corruption of it." In a moment of seriousness, Stewart said, "My mom was a teacher too, and she actually worked her [butt] off for not a lot of money."[80]

Stewart's Liberal Bias

The Republican governor of Wisconsin is but one of many conservatives Stewart has lambasted, or strongly criticized, on his show. In fact, over his many years on the air, Stewart's favorite topics for skewering have included former Bush administration officials, conservative talk show hosts like Glenn Beck and Bill O'Reilly, and Republican politicians like Representative John Boehner. Because many of Stewart's targets have been conservatives and Republicans, he is often accused of favoring liberal issues and Democrats. In fact, a 2010 study by the Center for Media and Public Affairs at George Mason University found that over a nine-month period, approximately 60 percent of *Daily Show* jokes targeted Republicans or conservatives.

Stewart claims he does not target Republicans, but rather those in power. Indeed, for all of Stewart's tenure on the show, the Republican Party has controlled at least one house of Congress, and from 2000 to 2008, the presidency. Also, Fox News—another frequent target of Stewart's, and one that tends to support conservative viewpoints—has the most cable news viewers. Stewart considers these fair targets, because they are the most powerful. As he explains: "I don't particularly think of ourselves as ideological here. ... I think we consider those with power and influence targets and those without it, not."[81] Former *Daily Show* cast member and fellow Comedy Central talk show host Stephen Colbert agrees, joking, "If liberals were in power it would be easier to attack them, but Republicans have the executive, legislative and judicial branches, so making fun of Democrats is like kicking a child, so it's just not worth it."[82]

Stewart often seeks out conservative guests and engages with them in extended and often repeated interviews. Conservative columnist William Kristol, former Republican governor and presidential candidate Mike Huckabee, and former Republican representative Newt Gingrich are among the show's regular guests. Republican senator John McCain has appeared on the show thirteen times, making him Stewart's second-most frequent guest. When former Republican spokesperson Cliff May was concerned about going on the liberal-leaning show, he called Kristol for advice. "Kristol told me: 'You'll be pleasantly surprised. He doesn't take cheap shots. Jon is smart. You'll do just fine,'"[83] May said. John Bolton, a staunch conservative and former ambassador the United Nations under Republican president George W. Bush, says: "He always gives you a chance to answer, which some people don't do. ... Stewart fundamentally wants to talk about the issues. That's what I want to do."[84]

Further proving Stewart chooses his targets based on their power rather than their politics is the fact that the George Mason

University study found that President Barack Obama, a Democrat, was the most frequent target for Stewart's satire in the nine months studied in 2010. Indeed, as Obama has established more of a record and pattern as president, Stewart has shown he is equally willing to go after a Democratic president as he was when the nation's chief executive was a Republican. For example, when the United States entered a military conflict in Libya in April 2011, Stewart repeatedly satirized Obama's lack of communication with the general public. Stewart has also cast Obama's actions as hypocritical by comparing the current president's leadership of

Stewart and Republican senator John McCain talk during a break in taping **The Daily Show** *in 2007. Although his show tends to be critical of Republicans and conservatives, Stewart frequently welcomes them as guests on his show.*

the U.S. military with his previous criticism of Bush's handling of the war in Iraq.

In his parodies of the nation's leaders, defense of unions and teachers, attacks on corporate greed, political corruption, or the failure of mainstream media to report on all of the above, Stewart has effectively positioned himself as a spokesperson for the American people. Yet he maintains he is not, as many have tried to call him, an activist, a leader, or the voice of a generation. "My mentality is more from the perspective of an angry guy at a bar,"[85] he says in his characteristic disarming style.

Chapter 5

Is Jon Stewart Still "Just a Comedian"?

As Jon Stewart and *The Daily Show* have become more successful and influential, many people question what role Stewart now plays. Is he still just a comedian, as he often claims? To some he has become much more: a journalist, an activist, and even someone who influences the passage of legislation within the federal government.

Stewart still maintains that he is a comedian first and foremost. He has responded to accusations that he is trying to be more by saying: "To say that comedians have to decide whether they're comedians or social commentators, uh … comedians do social commentary through comedy. That's how it's worked for thousands of years. I have not moved out of the comedian's box into the news box—the news box is moving towards me."[86]

A Rally to Restore Sanity

Although Stewart had previously blurred the line between entertainer and journalist, in the fall of 2010, he appeared to adopt the role of activist—or even political candidate. In October Stewart, along with Stephen Colbert, hosted a rally on the National Mall in Washington, D.C. Part comedy festival, part concert, and part parody of media-hyped political rallies, Stewart and Colbert pleaded for sanity in political discourse. They asked all those who "think shouting is annoying,

Stephen Colbert, left, and Stewart lead the Rally to Restore Sanity and/or Fear in October 2010. The event, held on the National Mall in Washington, D.C., was a mix of comedy, commentary, and music.

The Colbert Report

In 2005 *Daily Show* correspondent and cowriter Stephen Colbert left the program to begin hosting his own show. *The Colbert Report* is a similarly satirical news show that is based around the comic personality of Stephen Colbert, who uses the format to mock both the news and the egotistical cable news show hosts who report it.

The Colbert Report made news on its very first episode when Colbert coined the term *truthiness*, which refers to truths one instinctually knows or even prefers to be true. Dictionary publisher Merriam-Webster agreed with the power of this word and named it "word of the year" in 2006. Since then Colbert has traveled to Iraq, commissioned works of art, and coauthored a

*Former **Daily Show** correspondent Stephen Colbert became the star of his own show, **The Colbert Report**, in 2005.*

book with his staff under the guise of his show. Colbert also embraces the Internet. He encourages online action by his audience, such as modifying entries in the Internet-based encyclopedia *Wikipedia*, donating to real-life charities, or participating in various online contests.

Like Jon Stewart and *The Daily Show*, Stephen Colbert and *The Colbert Report* have won an Emmy Award, a Grammy Award, and a Peabody Award.

counterproductive, and terrible for your throat; who feel that the loudest voices shouldn't be the only ones that get heard; and who believe that the only time it's appropriate to draw a Hitler mustache on someone is when that person is actually Hitler"[87] to join them in an effort to tone down the national dialogue on political and social issues. The rally also featured a star-studded cast of musicians and a tightly choreographed mix of videos and live performances.

Approximately 215,000 people heard a largely ironic message that pleaded for a calmer, more rational approach to American politics by both liberals and conservatives. The audience brought thousands of homemade signs that expressed ironic political messages or pleas for more civil discourse. For example, one attendee brought a sign that ironically mocked the exaggerated, sometimes hysterical rhetoric (called "hyperbole") found at other political rallies and in the media. His sign read, "People who use hyperbole should be shot!" Others featured slogans such as "Civil is sexy!" and "It's a sad day when our politicians are comical and I have to take our comedians seriously." One sign, which parodied the trend of putting Hitler mustaches on images of political opponents, read: "I disagree with you, but I'm pretty sure you're not Hitler!"[88]

Though the event was peppered with humor, satire, and silliness, Stewart touched on many of the familiar themes from *The Daily Show* at the rally. He spoke about how politicians are overly partisan and chronically misrepresent both issues and their opponents. He also complained about the sensationalism and failure of news media. "If we amplify everything, we hear nothing," he said. "The press is our immune system. If we overreact to everything we actually get sicker."[89]

In his final speech, Stewart discussed how, despite the heightened rhetoric of politics and near-constant conflict shown in the media, Americans can be reasonable, work together, and get things done—and often do just that. Stewart said, "We live now in hard times, not end times. And we can have animus [hostility] and not be enemies."[90] He argued that extreme voices on both the left and the right must tone down their rhetoric so that reasonable debate and levelheadedness can prevail.

Stewart also argued that the media's portrayal of Americans as a people in constant political conflict is often untrue, and he praised Americans for working together all the time, every day. He illustrated his point with a metaphor, shown as a video of cars merging together to enter the Holland Tunnel, which joins his native New Jersey with his new home and workplace of New York City. As the cars merge into the tunnel, Stewart muses that the drivers are probably very different and even wrestle their own internal conflicts and compromises. His speech reaches its climax not with an impassioned address, but with calm appreciation of the little, yet important, compromises that Americans make every day:

These millions of cars must somehow find a way to squeeze one by one into a mile long 30 foot wide tunnel carved underneath a mighty river. Carved, by the way, by people who I'm sure had their differences. And they do it. Concession by concession. You go. Then I'll go. ... Because we know instinctively as a people that if we are to get through the darkness and back into the light we have to work together. And the truth is, there will always be darkness. And sometimes the light at the end of the tunnel isn't the promised land. Sometimes it's just New Jersey. But we do it anyway, together.[91]

Response to His Rally

Response to the Rally to Restore Sanity ranged from glowing praise, to disappointment, to harsh criticism. Among those who viewed it as a success were CNN's John P. Avalon, who wrote:

For all the humor and affirmation, the Restore Sanity rally ultimately had a serious point that will apply when the election is over—namely, that we have to work together to solve problems, but our polarized [divided] politics and the partisan [biased] media are stopping our ability to reason together as Americans. ... The rally's size and enthusiasm was evidence of a growing demand for something different—an alternative to predictable talking points and the partisan spin cycle, a desire for humor and honesty, independence and integrity. It is both an opportunity and an obligation.[92]

Student Emerson Brooking, writing in the newspaper the *Daily Pennsylvanian*, agreed with Avalon. "For a few hours on a beautiful

Many of the approximately 215,000 people who attended the Rally to Restore Sanity and/or Fear carried signs in support of Stewart's call to end the damaging rhetoric that had come to dominate politics in the United States.

October day, Americans were able to take a step back from the rhetoric that splits our country and a media that makes it worse," wrote Brooking. "The rally was not a call to action, but it will most certainly stand as a call to reason."[93]

Another sign of the rally's success was its far-reaching, even global, appeal. The *Christian Science Monitor* reported that in addition to the hundreds of thousands people who rallied in Washington, there were more than 1,160 mini-rallies held in over eighty countries. Also, following the rally, at least one of the media personalities generally criticized by Stewart changed his ways. On the Monday after the rally, MSNBC talk show host Keith Olbermann suspended a segment of his show called "The Worst Person in the World." Olbermann did not say that the change was a direct result of Stewart or the Rally to Restore Sanity, but he did agree that the "tone needs to change."[94]

Others were not as impressed, however. Liberal comedian Bill Maher, who also focuses on politics and current events, blasted

Stewart for making it sound as if conservatives and liberals are equally unreasonable. As Maher put it, "The big mistake of modern media has been this notion of balance for balance's sake, that the left is just as violent and cruel as the right, that unions are just as powerful as corporations, that reverse racism is just as damaging as racism." In an extended critique of Stewart's assertion that both political sides equally overstate, exaggerate, and demonize one another, Maher gave little value to Stewart's claim that "the national conversation is dominated by people on the right who believe Obama is a socialist and people on the left who believe 9/11 was an inside job." Maher countered, "I can't name any Democratic leaders who think 9/11 was an inside job, but Republican leaders who think Obama's a socialist? That's all of them!" Maher's conclusion was that Stewart should not encourage Americans to give equal value to all arguments simply for the sake of appearing balanced. As Maher put it, "Two opposing sides don't necessarily have two compelling arguments."[95] AlterNet columnist Daniel Denvir agreed. "Yelling is not just a matter of loud noise expelled through the human throat. It matters what's being yelled," he said. "Jon Stewart's Million Moderate March draws a false equivalence [likeness] between right-wing propagandists, and people on the left who rightly lashed out against [former President George W.] Bush."[96]

Presidential Pit Stop

Although many panned the Rally to Restore Sanity or were frustrated with its premise, it still made headlines. Also making headlines in the fall of 2010 was Stewart's impressive guest list. In its first few years, *The Daily Show* struggled to attract top-level officials or political insiders to the program. Over the years, however, Stewart's guest list has become increasingly populated by America's most powerful political, corporate, and media leaders. Numerous heads of state, including former presidents Bill Clinton and Jimmy Carter, and the leaders of other nations have sat down to talk with Stewart. Vice presidents and numerous senators, congresspeople, presidential cabinet members,

President Barack Obama is interviewed by Stewart in October 2010. The appearance marked the first time a sitting president was a guest on **The Daily Show.**

corporate founders, top-rated news anchors, and other important personalities regularly appear on his show, too. *The Daily Show*'s impressive list of guests has caused *Newsweek* to describe it as "the coolest pit stop on television"[97] and has highlighted Stewart's development as a person of importance and a reputable interviewer.

The most high-profile guest to date appeared on October 27, 2010, when *The Daily Show* hosted President Barack Obama. Although Stewart had interviewed former presidents before, it was the first time a sitting president appeared on the show. The timing of the appearance was also significant: It was just days

A Private Man

Jon Stewart is a private man who rarely discusses his personal life. When off camera he enjoys a fairly quiet family life with his wife, Tracey, their son, Nathan (born in 2004), and their daughter, Maggie (born in 2006). He also shares his home with two pit bull terriers and a cat. Stewart prefers his personal time to be focused on bonding with his family. "When I'm at home, I'm locked in and I'm ready to go." He said, "We don't watch the show. We don't watch the news. We don't do any of that stuff. I sit down, I play Barbies. And sometimes the kids will come home and play with me."

Quoted in *Fresh Air*. "Jon Stewart: The Most Trusted Name in Fake News." NPR, October 4, 2010. www.npr.org/templates/story/story.php?storyId=130321994.

before the 2010 midterm elections. That Obama had selected *The Daily Show* for an appearance during this busy and politically strategic time helped legitimize Stewart.

Stewart used the show's entire thirty minutes to interview the president. He maintained a comfortable, casual tone, but also asked some tough questions and made pointed statements. For example, Stewart contrasted Obama's soaring campaign speeches with the more discouraging realities of his presidency, saying, "You ran on very high rhetoric, 'hope and change,' and the Democrats this year seem to be running on 'please, baby, one more chance.'" He described some of the president's efforts on issues such as health care as "timid," but also referred to the commander in chief as "dude."[98]

Throughout the interview, Stewart maintained the environment that has encouraged others to view him as a serious interviewer. He disagreed with the president on certain issues, but the two also joked, respectfully. Most of all, the Obama interview clearly established Stewart as part of a select group of people who can access a sitting president.

Comedy for a Cause: The 9/11 First Responders

Stewart again went beyond the traditional boundaries of comedy in December 2010, when he championed a government proposal to provide health care benefits for 9/11 first responders (the first emergency personnel to arrive at Ground Zero after the attacks). In this story Stewart appeared as more of a traditional journalist, or even a political activist, as he advocated for passage of a bill that would take care of police officers and firefighters who became sick after working at the September 11 terrorist attack sites.

Throughout 2010, Democratic members of the Senate tried to pass a bill, called the Zadroga Bill, that proposed the establishment of a multibillion-dollar fund to pay for health care when insurance or workers' compensation ran out for the September 11 workers. However, political disagreements caused Republican senators to block votes on the bill, and by December it seemed

A former worker at Ground Zero attends a press conference held by New York City mayor Michael Bloomberg to voice support for the Zadroga Bill. Stewart used his show as a platform to publicize the bill and the politics that threatened its approval.

the Zadroga Bill would not pass. Dismayed, Stewart launched a two-pronged attack in response.

In the final *Daily Show* episode of 2010, Stewart called the political deadlock "an outrageous abdication [handing over] of our responsibility to those who were most heroic on 9/11." He went after Republicans for using 9/11-related patriotism when it was politically expedient for them, but for failing to support care for the heroes of 9/11. Next he criticized the lack of coverage of the topic in the mainstream media, noting, "None of the three broadcast networks have mentioned any of this on their evening newscasts for two and a half months." To drive home how outrageous this was, Stewart cut to a clip of a newscaster using prime airtime to report on iTunes music sales. Stewart sarcastically noted, "Although to be fair, it's not every day that Beatles songs come to iTunes. Music? For sale on the Internet? Wha...?" After especially scathing criticism of Fox News, Stewart noted that the only network to air a full report on the stalled Zadroga Bill was Arabic news channel Al-Jazeera, "the same network that [9/11 terrorist mastermind] Osama Bin Ladin sends his mix tapes to." Exclaimed Stewart, "This is insane!"[99]

America Takes Note

Stewart then devoted the remainder of his show to interviews about the Zadroga Bill. For one segment Stewart hosted a panel of four 9/11 first responders who worked at Ground Zero immediately following the terrorist attacks. On his panel were New York City police officers and firefighters who had gotten sick with cancer or were otherwise injured from exposure to toxic chemicals present where they were involved in rescue and cleanup. Stewart allowed the men to speak openly about their problems securing health care for the illnesses related to their work. Then he showed a video of a Republican senator giving a tearful speech on the same day that Republicans blocked a vote to pay for the health care of workers like Stewart's guests—except the speech was an emotional farewell to a Republican colleague who had retired. The panel wasted no time in noting the hypocrisy and insensitivity. "He said something very important," one firefighter noted. "He's going to

Award Winner and Awards Show Host

Jon Stewart and *The Daily Show* team are no strangers to awards shows. Together they have won two Peabody Awards for excellence in broadcasting, fourteen Emmy Awards, and a Grammy Award for the audio book recording of *America (The Book)*.

Stewart has also served as an awards show host. In 2001 and 2002 he hosted the Grammy Awards show for the National Academy of Recording Arts and Sciences. In 2006 and 2008 Stewart hosted the Academy Awards show, in which the Academy of Motion Picture Arts and Sciences gives awards for achievement in the filmmaking industry.

watch his friend walk out of the Senate chambers, and unfortunately that's more than a New York City firefighter can say about 343 of his brothers who can't walk anymore."[100]

In the final segment of the show, Stewart interviewed Fox News contributor and former Republican presidential candidate Mike Huckabee about the Zadroga Bill. Huckabee initially tried to explain the Republican reasons for blocking the vote, but after Stewart rebutted his arguments, he quickly changed course and said, "Every Republican should vote for this bill."[101]

The next day, the rest of the media changed their tune. Fox News ran segments that supported Stewart's actions, and Shepard Smith, a Fox News anchor, even called Stewart "absolutely right."[102] ABC News covered the issue for the first time and quoted from the previous day's *Daily Show* episode. On the Internet, videos of Stewart's coverage of the 9/11 first responders bill went viral. Clips were viewed hundreds of thousands of times on Comedy Central's website, YouTube, and other sites.

Most importantly, politicians in Washington took notice. On December 22, less than two weeks after Stewart's program,

Congress passed and President Obama signed a compromise on the Zadroga Bill, which finally established a government-funded health care provision for 9/11 workers. The night before the bill passed through Congress, White House Press Secretary Robert Gibbs told reporters that Stewart had "put awareness around the legislation,"[103] and brought it into focus for the media.

"Forever Indebted to Jon"

Stewart was roundly praised for his efforts. MSNBC political commentator Rachel Maddow thanked Stewart for providing "a great service," adding, "Despite everybody else's inability to focus on a matter for any significant amount of time, he refused to stop covering the 9/11 first responders bill."[104] John Feal, the activist

New York City mayor Michael Bloomberg, standing at the podium, is surrounded by other New York politicians as he expresses his approval of the passage of the Zadroga Bill in December 2010. Bloomberg was one of several prominent people who praised Stewart.

who connected Stewart with the first responders who appeared as guests on *The Daily Show*, said that Jon Stewart "literally shamed conventional media and the U.S. government into doing the right thing."[105] Said Kenny Specht, one of the firefighters on Stewart's panel, "I'll forever be indebted to Jon because of what he did."[106] *Slate* writer Christopher Beam even declared that Stewart was stepping "onto the political playing field."[107]

New York mayor Michael Bloomberg also praised Stewart's efforts, and the National September 11 Memorial & Museum appointed Stewart to its board of directors. Said memorial president Joe Daniels, "He has taken a definitive stance on so many issues that relate directly to our organization's mission of commemoration and education."[108] Stewart, who was honored, joked, "I'm hoping to help in any way I can offer. I am like their intern."[109]

Others, however, were not as impressed. Blogging for the conservative news outfit the *Weekly Standard*, John McCormack argued that Stewart's show "may have been triumph of advocacy, [but] it was a failure of journalism" because he "didn't really try to understand why Republicans objected to the bill."[110] Interestingly, this criticism revealed the *Weekly Standard*'s expectation for Stewart to follow traditional journalistic practices. Others downplayed Stewart's involvement in the matter, saying the bill was actually close to passage and that Stewart just happened to discuss it at the right moment. Yet even critics acknowledged that Stewart had stepped out of his role as a comedian and become a force to be reckoned with, or at least discussed.

America's Most Trusted Newscaster

As a result of Stewart's ever-expanding audience, his standout social commentary, his quality reporting, his ability to access the world's most powerful and important people, and his ability to generate news and even influence the passage of legislation, many regard Stewart as a social and political force in his own right. By the end of 2010 Stewart had used his position as a critic who calls out jokes from the balcony to cement himself as one of the most powerful voices in the media.

Walter Cronkite, left, and Edward R. Murrow were prominent news broadcasters who earned great public respect for their professionalism. Some have compared Stewart's level of influence and trust among his viewers to that which Cronkite and Murrow achieved during their careers.

In fact, Stewart has increasingly earned comparisons to the famous journalists Edward R. Murrow and Walter Cronkite. Both Murrow and Cronkite are famous for shaping public perceptions through focused reporting of controversial subjects. Cronkite anchored the *CBS Evening News* for nearly twenty years, while Murrow was a successful radio and television journalist.

In the 1950s Murrow achieved lasting fame through his use of journalism to expose former senator Joseph McCarthy. McCarthy had used his political power to root out suspected Communists from American society, but Murrow's reporting on these events dramatically turned the public against the senator. On March 9, 1954, Murrow aired a broadcast that pieced together film clips and audio of Senator McCarthy hypocritically and fanatically abusing his power in a way that was damaging American society. The public overwhelmingly agreed with Murrow's perspective, and McCarthy fell from power. Cronkite, too, was so respected by his peers and the public that his Vietnam War–era newscasts are often credited with turning the tide of public opinion—or at least officially marking its turn—from supportive to antiwar.

Stewart's contemporary use of audio and video clips to expose hypocrisy, bias, and corruption echoes Murrow's techniques. Stewart also embodies both Murrow's and Cronkite's willingness to report passionately on stories that were of personal importance to them or stories they felt were particularly important for the nation to understand.

For years Walter Cronkite was America's most trusted journalist. When he died in 2009, *Time* magazine asked its readers whom they trusted most as a newscaster, now that Cronkite was no longer alive. *Time's* readers overwhelmingly chose Jon Stewart. "What Cronkite and Murrow did was they stepped out of their traditional role of objectivity and had an opinion about something," says C.W. Anderson, assistant professor of media culture at the College of Staten Island. "And when they did that, people noticed, people listened. Jon Stewart always has an opinion. But for Jon Stewart, when he steps outside of his comic role and behaves seriously, people listen."[111]

In the current era there may simply be too many voices on cable news for any one person to come across as the "official" newscaster of a generation. However, as television producer Steve Rosenbaum notes, "Stewart has positioned himself as the curator of the day's news."[112] Stewart is unique in his role as a trusted filter who combs through the day's news and reveals what should be understood about not only the events, but the media's portrayal of it. As Rosenbaum puts it, "Jon Stewart isn't a newsman, a reporter, or a correspondent. But he is an honest broker of ideas in a time when a curator is needed."[113]

The *Time* magazine poll did not impress everyone: Whet Moser, a writer for the *Chicago Reader*, was quick to point out that the poll was unscientific, and that Stewart's rise has coincided with the decline of traditional media. As Moser put it, "Stewart is gaining our trust, but at the same time [the mainstream media has] done much to lose it."[114] Stewart would likely be the first to agree. After all, Americans may trust him for the news, but this might simply be because the major news networks have lost their viewers' trust—and that is Jon Stewart's favorite topic of all.

Introduction: From News Mocker to News Maker

1. Quoted in Chris Smith. "America Is a Joke." *New York*, September 12, 2010. http://nymag.com/arts/tv/profiles/68086.
2. Quoted in *Bill Moyers Journal*. "Transcript." PBS, April 27, 2007. www.pbs.org/moyers/journal/04272007/transcript4.html.
3. Quoted in Smith. "America Is a Joke."
4. Quoted in *The Rachel Maddow Show*. MSNBC, November 11, 2010. Television.
5. Quoted in *Fresh Air*. "Jon Stewart: The Most Trusted Name in Fake News." NPR, October 4, 2010. www.npr.org/templates/story/story.php?storyId=130321994.

Chapter 1: The Little Kid Who Got Big Laughs

6. Quoted in Maria Speidel. "Prince of Cool Air." *People*, April 4, 1994. www.people.com/people/archive/article/0,,20107783,00.html.
7. Quoted in Curt Schleier. "Timing Is Everything." *Jewish Week*, October 9, 1998, p. 33.
8. Quoted in Marshall Owens. "Jon Stewart Recalls Life as a Local Boy." *Daily Princetonian*, March 23, 2000. www.dailyprincetonian.com/2000/03/23/490.
9. Quoted in Ed Condran. "Jon Stewart Is More than a Funny Guy." *Bucks County (PA) Courier Times*, May 4, 2002. http://jon.happyjoyfun.net/tran/2002/02_0504bucks.html.
10. Quoted in Rob Tannenbaum. "How I Became a Man." *Details*, January 1999. http://jon.happyjoyfun.net/tran/1999/99_0100details.html.
11. Quoted in Louis B. Hobson. "Jon Stewart's Cookin' Now." *Calgary Sun*, June 26, 1999. http://jam.canoe.ca/Movies/Artists/S/Stewart_Jon/1999/06/24/761984.html.

12. Quoted in Cindy Pearlman. "Must Be Moving On." *Chicago Sun Times*, June 20, 1999. www.highbeam.com/doc/1P2-4487791.html?key=01-42161A527E1C1061140D0B1E4A3F593C3B4F36602F2A3342720F0B61651A617E137119731B7B51.

13. Quoted in Allison Adato. "Anchor Astray." *George*, May 2000. http://home.earthlink.net/~aladato/anchor.html.

14. Quoted in Jeremy Gillick and Nona Gorilovskaya. "Meet Jon Stuart Leibowitz (aka) Jon Stewart: The Wildly Zeitgeisty Daily Show Host." *Moment*, November/December 2008. www.momentmag.com/Exclusive/2008/12/JonStewart.html.

15. Quoted in Gillick and Gorilovskaya. "Meet Jon Stuart Lieibowitz (aka) Jon Stewart."

16. Quoted in Gillick and Gorilovskaya. "Meet Jon Stuart Lieibowitz (aka) Jon Stewart."

17. Quoted in Chris Weidman. "WM's Most Famous Alum, Jon Stewart, Spun Soccer into Success." *Williamsburg Yorktown (VA) Daily*, October 25, 2010. www.wydaily.com/local-news/5259-wms-most-famous-alum-jon-stewart-spun-soccer-into-success.html.

18. Quoted in Ben Domenech. "Jon Stewart: The SIN Interview." Student Information Network, College of William & Mary, April 26, 2002. http://natspaz.tripod.com/thejonstewartshrine/id29.html.

19. Quoted in Meghan Williams. "Jon Stewart, Host of "The Daily Show." Class of '84 Comedian, Alumnus Returns to College for Q&A Session." *Flat Hat*, November 1, 2002. www.greekchat.com/gcforums/showthread.php?t=26527.

20. Quoted in Steve Kroft. "Jon Stewart's Rise to Stardom." *60 Minutes*. April 22, 2001. http://jon.happyjoyfun.net/tran/2001/01_0423sixtymin.html.

21. Jon Stewart. "Jon Stewart's ('84) Commencement Address." *William & Mary News*, May 20, 2004. http://web.wm.edu/news/archive/index.php?id=3650.

22. Quoted in Tad Friend. "Is It Funny Yet?" *New Yorker*, February 11, 2002, p. 28.

23. Quoted in Brooke Gladstone, *NPR Weekend*. "Jon Stewart." October 3, 1998.

Chapter 2: Chasing the Dream

24. Quoted in Friend. "Is It Funny Yet?," p. 30
25. Quoted in Barry Koltnow. "Jon Stewart Lives by His Sharp Wit." *Dallas Morning News*, July 9, 1999. http://jon. happyjoyfun.net/tran/1999/99_0709dallas.html.
26. Quoted in Koltnow. "Jon Stewart Lives by His Sharp Wit."
27. Quoted in *Bloomberg Game Changers*. "Episode 3: Jon Stewart." Bloomberg Television, October 22, 2010. www. bloomberg.com/news/2010-10-22/bloomberg-game-changers-jon-stewart.html.
28. Quoted in *Bloomberg Game Changers*. "Episode 3."
29. Quoted in Scott Williams. "Comedian Jon Stewart Enters the Talk Show Lists." Associated Press, October 22, 1993. http://jon.happyjoyfun.net/tran/1990/93_1022ap.html.
30. Quoted in *Newsmakers*. "Jon Stewart." Gale Biography in Context, March 1, 2001.
31. Quoted in Chris Smith. "Jon Gone." *New York*, July 10, 1995, p. 17.
32. Quoted in *O: The Oprah Magazine*. "Oprah Talks to Jon Stewart." June 15, 2005. www.oprah.com/omagazine/ Oprah-Interviews-Jon-Stewart/6.
33. Jon Stewart. *Naked Pictures of Famous People*. New York, Perennial, 1998, p. 56.
34. Stewart. *Naked Pictures of Famous People*, p. 141.
35. Tom Faucett. "Review: Naked Pictures of Famous People." *CNN Entertainment*, April 20, 1999. http://articles.cnn.com/1999-04-20/entertainment/9904_20_naked.pictures_1_jon-stewart-martha-stewart-famous-people?_s=PM:books.
36. Quoted in A.J. Jacobs. "Jonny on the Spot." *Entertainment Weekly*, January 8, 1999. www.ew.com/ew/article/0,,273992_2,00.html.
37. Quoted in Seth Margolis. "SIGNOFF; Enough News to Keep 'Em Rolling." *New York Times*, January 10, 1999. http:// query.nytimes.com/gst/fullpage.html?res=9A0DE3D81631 F933A25752C0A96F958260http://query.nytimes.com/gst/

fullpage.html?res=9A0DE3D81631F933A25752C0A96F95
8260&scp=1&sq=%22jon+stewart%22+%22daily+show%
22&st=nyt.

38. Quoted in Stephen Thompson. "*The Daily Show's* Stephen Colbert, Rob Corddry, Ed Helms and Mo Rocco." *A.V. Club*, January 22, 2003. www.avclub.com/articles/the-daily-shows-stephen-colbert-rob-corddry-ed-hel,13795.

39. Peter Keepnews. "Late-Night Hosts in Search of Their Niches." *New York Times*, October 3, 1999. www.nytimes.com/1999/10/03/arts/television-radio-late-night-hosts-in-search-of-their-niches.html?src=pm.

40. Quoted in Smith. "America Is a Joke."

41. *The Daily Show with Jon Stewart*. Comedy Central, May 25, 1999. Television.

42. *The Daily Show with Jon Stewart*. Comedy Central, December 16, 1999. Television.

43. Friend. "Is It Funny Yet?," p. 31.

Chapter 3: *The Daily Show* Grows Up

44. *The Daily Show with Jon Stewart*. Comedy Central. November 8, 2000. Television.

45. Quoted in Mike Flaherty. "Stewart Has Real Flair for Fake News." *Variety*, January 20, 2009. www.variety.com/article/VR1117998822?refcatid=3523&printerfriendly=true.

46. Peabody Awards. "The Daily Show with Jon Stewart: Indecision 2000." www.peabody.uga.edu/winners/details.php?id=1268.

47. *The Daily Show with Jon Stewart*. Comedy Central, September 20, 2001. Television.

48. *The Daily Show with Jon Stewart*, September 20, 2001. Television.

49. *The Daily Show with Jon Stewart*, September 20, 2001. Television.

50. Peabody Awards. "The Daily Show with Jon Stewart."

51. Quoted in CNN.com. "CNN Crossfire: Jon Stewart's America." Transcript. October 15, 2004. http://transcripts.cnn.com/TRANSCRIPTS/0410/15/cf.01.html.

52. Quoted in CNN.com. "CNN Crossfire."

53. Quoted in CNN.com. "CNN Crossfire."

54. Quoted in CNN.com. "CNN Crossfire."

55. Quoted in Thomas Goetz. "Reinventing Television." Interview. *Wired*, September 2005. www.wired.com/wired/archive/13.09/stewart.html.

56. Alessandra Stanley. "No Jokes or Spin. It's Time (Gasp) to Talk." *New York Times*, October 20, 2004. www.nytimes.com/2004/10/20/arts/television/20watc.html.

57. Dan Kennedy. "Media Log in the Crossfire." *Boston Phoenix*, October 18, 2004. http://medialogarchives.blogspot.com/2004_10_01_archive.html.

58. Quoted in Bill Carter. "CNN Will Cancel 'Crossfire' and Cut Ties to Commentator." *New York Times*, January 6, 2005. www.nytimes.com/2005/01/06/business/media/06crossfire.html.

59. Quoted in Howard Kurtz. "Carlson & 'Crossfire,' Exit Stage Left & Right." *Washington Post*, January 6, 2005. www.washingtonpost.com/wp-dyn/articles/A52274-2005Jan6.html.

60. Annenberg Public Policy Center. "Daily Show Viewers Knowledgeable About Presidential Campaign, National Annenberg Election Survey Shows." September 21, 2004. www.annenbergpublicpolicycenter.org/Downloads/Political_Communication/naes/2004_03_late-night-knowledge-2_9-21_pr.pdf.

61. Quoted in Annenberg Public Policy Center. "Daily Show Viewers Knowledgeable About Presidential Campaign, National Annenberg Election Survey Shows."

62. Quoted in Annenberg Public Policy Center. "Daily Show Viewers Knowledgeable About Presidential Campaign, National Annenberg Election Survey Shows."

63. *The Daily Show with Jon Stewart*. Comedy Central, September 29, 2004. Television.

Chapter 4: The Voice of the People

64. Eric Alterman. "Is Jon Stewart Our Ed Murrow? Maybe. ..." *Nation*, March 26, 2009. www.thenation.com/article/jon-stewart- our-ed-murrow-maybe.

65. David Smith. "America Cheers as Satirist, Jon Stewart, Delivers Knockout Blow to TV Finance Gurus." *Guardian* (UK), March 15, 2009. www.guardian.co.uk/world/2009/mar/15/usa-tv-jon-stewart-economy.

66. John Lott. "Jon Stewart Deceptively Edits Footage in Story." *John Lott's Website*, January 31, 2011. http://johnrlott. blogspot.com/2011/01/jon-stewart-deceptively-edits-footage.html.

67. Michael Moynihan. "There Is No Truth." *Reason*, October 17, 2007. http://reason.com/archives/2007/10/17/there-is-no-truth.

68. *The Daily Show with Jon Stewart.* Comedy Central, March 12, 2009. Television.

69. Nikki Finke. "WGA Reminds Returning Jay and Conan: No Monologues." *Deadline.com*, December 17, 2007. www. deadline.com/2007/12/wga-reminds-returning-jay-conan-dont-write-monologues.

70. *The Daily Show with Jon Stewart.* Comedy Central, March 4, 2009. Television.

71. *The Daily Show with Jon Stewart*, March 4, 2009. Television.

72. *The Daily Show with Jon Stewart*, March 12, 2009. Television.

73. *The Daily Show with Jon Stewart*, March 12, 2009. Television.

74. *The Daily Show with Jon Stewart*, March 12, 2009. Television.

75. *The Daily Show with Jon Stewart*, March 12, 2009. Television.

76. David Folkenflik. "On '*Daily Show*,' Stewart, Cramer Get Serious." National Public Radio, March 13, 2009. www. npr.org/templates/story/story.php?storyId=101888064&ft=1&f=1057.

77. Mark A. Perigard. "Jim Cramer vs. Jon Stewart: When Blowhards Collide." *Boston Herald*, March 13, 2009. www. bostonherald.com/entertainment/television/general/view. bg?articleid=1158296.

78. Alterman. "Is Jon Stewart Our Ed Murrow?"

79. *The Daily Show with Jon Stewart.* Comedy Central, March 10, 2011. Television.

80. *The Daily Show with Jon Stewart.* Comedy Central, February 28, 2011. Television.

81. Quoted in Gary Younge. "Such a Tease." Interview. *Guardian* (UK), October 1, 2005. www.guardian.co.uk/media/2005/oct/01/usa.television.

82. Quoted in Elana Berkowitz and Amy Schiller. "Five Minutes with Stephen Colbert." Interview. Campus Progress, July 11, 2005. www.campusprogress.org/articles/stephen_colbert.

83. Quoted in Jacob Gershman. "Why Neoconservative Pundits Love Jon Stewart." *New York Magazine*, August 9, 2009. http://nymag.com/daily/intel/2009/08/why_conservative_pundits_love.html.

84. Quoted in Gershman. "Why Neoconservative Pundits Love Jon Stewart."

85. Quoted in Jim Wallis. "The Truth Smirks." Interview. *Sojourners*, July 2009. www.sojo.net/index.cfm?action=magazine.article&issue=soj0907&article=the-truth-smirks.

Chapter 5: Is Jon Stewart Still "Just a Comedian"?

86. *The Daily Show with Jon Stewart*. Comedy Central, April 20, 2010. Television.

87. Rally to Restore Sanity. Home page. September 9, 2010. www.rallytorestoresanity.com.

88. Quoted in Katla McGlynn. "The Funniest Signs from the Rally to Restore Sanity and/or Fear." *Huffington Post*, October 30, 2010. www.huffingtonpost.com/2010/10/30/the-funniest-signs-at-the_n_776490.html#s169371&title=Nope.

89. Quoted in Liz Brown. "Rally to Restore Sanity—Jon Stewart's Closing Speech (Full Text)." *Examiner.com*, October 30, 2010. www.examiner.com/celebrity-in-national/rally-to-restore-sanity-jon-stewart-s-closing-speech-full-text.

90. Quoted in Brown. "Rally to Restore Sanity—Jon Stewart's Closing Speech (Full Text)."

91. Quoted in Brown. "Rally to Restore Sanity—Jon Stewart's Closing Speech (Full Text)."

92. John P. Avalon. "Stewart Rally's Point—Don't Divide Us." CNN.com, November 1, 2010. www.cnn.com/2010/OPINION/10/31/avlon.rally.sanity/index.html?iref=allsearch.

93. Emerson Brooking. "Rally to Restore Sanity: The Joke's On Us." *Daily Pennsylvanian*, November 2, 2010. www.dailypennsylvanian.com/article/southern-comfort-rally-restore-sanity-joke-s-us.

94. Quoted in Aliya Shahid. "Keith Olbermann Drops 'Worst Persons in the World' Segment on MSNBC After Jon Stewart Rally." *New York Daily News*, November 2, 2010. www.nydailynews.com/news/politics/2010/11/02/2010-11-02_keith_olbermann_drops_worst_person_in_the_world_segment_on_msnbc_after_jon_stewa.html.

95. Bill Maher. *Politically Incorrect*. ABC, November 6, 2010. Television.

96. Daniel Denvir. "Hey Jon Stewart, WTF? How Can You Compare Crazy, Lying Right-Wingers to Progressives?" AlterNet, September 23, 2010. www.alternet.org/media/148254/hey_jon_stewart,_wtf_how_can_you_compare_crazy,_lying_right-wingers_to_progressives?utm_source=feedblitz&utm_medium=FeedBlitzRss&utm_campaign=alternet.

97. Mark Peyser. "Jon Stewart: Red, White & Funny." *Newsweek*, December 28, 2003. www.newsweek.com/2003/12/28/red-white-funny.html.

98. *The Daily Show with Jon Stewart*. Comedy Central, October 27, 2010. Television.

99. *The Daily Show with Jon Stewart*. Comedy Central, December 16, 2010. Television.

100. *The Daily Show with Jon Stewart*, December 16, 2010. Television.

101. *The Daily Show with Jon Stewart*, December 16, 2010. Television.

102. Quoted in Brian Stelter. "Jon Stewart, the Advocate, on the 9/11 Health Bill." *New York Times*, December 17, 2010. http://mediadecoder.blogs.nytimes.com/2010/12/17/jon-stewart-the-advocate-on-the-911-health-bill.

103. Quoted in Lucy Madison. "White House Lauds Jon Stewart for Pushing Passage of 9/11 Health Bill." CBSNews.com, December 21, 2010. www.cbsnews.com/8301-503544_162-20026333-503544.html.

104. *The Rachel Maddow Show*. MSNBC, December 17, 2010. Television.

105. Quoted in Christopher Beam. "No Joke: By Pushing for the 9/11 First Responders Health Bill, Jon Stewart Steps onto the Political Playing Field." *Slate*, December 20, 2010. www.slate.com/id/2278625.

106. Quoted in Bill Carter and Brian Stelter. "In 'Daily Show' Role on 9/11 Bill, Echoes of Murrow." *New York Times*, December 27, 2010. www.nytimes.com/2010/12/27/business/media/27stewart.html?pagewanted=1&_r=3&src=twt&twt=nytimes.

107. Beam. "No Joke."

108. Quoted in Laura Batchelor. "Jon Stewart Named to 9/11 Memorial and Museum Board of Directors." CNN.com, January 28, 2011. http://articles.cnn.com/2011-01-28/us/new.york.stewart.9.11_1_memorial-and-museum-jon-stewart-health-bill?_s=PM:US.

109. Quoted in Batchelor. "Jon Stewart Named to 9/11 Memorial and Museum Board of Directors."

110. John McCormack. "Jon Stewart's 9/11 Demagoguery." *Weekly Standard*, December 22, 2010. www.weeklystandard.com/blogs/jon-stewarts-911-demagoguery_524806.html.

111. Quoted in Sheila Marikar. "Jon Stewart: Edward R. Murrow Incarnate, or Something Else Entirely?" December 27, 2010. http://abcnews.go.com/Entertainment/jon-stewart-edward-murrow-incarnate/story?id=12485707&page=2.

112. Steve Rosenbaum. "Is Jon Stewart the Walter Cronkite of This Generation?" *Huffington Post*, July 6, 2010. www.huffingtonpost.com/steve-rosenbaum/who-is-the-walter-cronkit_b_636877.html.

113. Rosenbaum. "Is Jon Stewart the Walter Cronkite of This Generation?"

114. Whet Moser. "Walter Cronkite, Jon Stewart, and Trust." *Chicago Reader*, July 24, 2009. www.chicagoreader.com/TheBlog/archives/2009/07/24/walter-cronkite-jon-stewart-and-trust.

1962

Jon Stewart is born on November 28, 1962.

1971

Stewart's father leaves the family, and his parents divorce shortly thereafter.

1980

Graduates from Lawrence High School third in his class.

1984

Graduates from the College of William & Mary with a degree in psychology.

1987

Makes his debut as a stand-up comedian at the Bitter End in Greenwich Village and changes his name from Jon Leibowitz to Jon Stewart.

1988

Opens for pop singer Sheena Easton in Las Vegas.

1991

Cohosts Comedy Central's *Short Attention Span Theater*.

1993

Hosts *The Jon Stewart Show*, but it is canceled after only a year on the air.

1994

Makes his film debut as a Rollerblade skater in the film *Mixed Nuts*.

1996

Hosts an HBO stand-up comedy special called *Jon Stewart: Unleavened*; signs with David Letterman's production company, *Worldwide Pants*; meets future wife Tracey McShane.

1998

Publishes *Naked Pictures of Famous People*.

1999

Begins hosting *The Daily Show with Jon Stewart* on Comedy Central; appears in the movie *Big Daddy* with comedic actor Adam Sandler; makes *People* magazine's "50 Most Beautiful People" list.

2000

Stewart and *The Daily Show* crew cover the 2000 presidential elections, attending both conventions and doing a special live show on election night; *The Daily Show* receives a Peabody Award for its *Indecision 2000* coverage; Stewart and McShane marry.

2001

Hosts the Grammy Awards show; *The Daily Show* wins its first Emmy; Stewart gives a heartfelt nine-minute monologue on September 20, on his first show after the 9/11 terrorist attack on the World Trade Center.

2002

Hosts the Grammy Awards show for the second time; the film *Death to Smoochy* is released.

2003

Senator John Edwards officially announces his presidential candidacy on *The Daily Show*.

2004

The Daily Show covers the 2004 presidential election, again attending both conventions and hosting a live election night special; Stewart interviews several key politicians, including Senator John McCain, past president Bill Clinton, and Democratic nominee John Kerry; *The Daily Show* garners a second Peabody Award for election coverage; Stewart captures the media's attention when he crosses swords with *Crossfire* host Tucker Carlson, who is later fired in part because of Stewart's appearance on his show; Stewart publishes best-selling mock textbook, *America (The Book): A Citizen's Guide to Democracy Inaction*; Stewart's first child, Nathan, is born in July.

2005

The Daily Show moves to a bigger studio with a new set; Stewart helps Stephen Colbert launch his spin-off show, *The Colbert Report*.

2006

Hosts the Academy Awards show; Stewart's second child, Maggie, is born in February.

2008

Stewart hosts the Academy Awards show for the second time; *The Daily Show* covers the 2008 elections; Stewart interviews future president Barack Obama just a few days before the election.

2009

Has much publicized feud with *Mad Money* host Jim Cramer in March; calls former president Harry Truman a war criminal but then apologizes.

2010

The Daily Show wins its fourteenth Emmy Award; *The Daily Show* makes *Time* magazine's "100 Best TV Shows of All-Time" list; Stewart is named "Most Influential Man of the Year" by *AskMen.com*; publishes *Earth (The Book): A Visitor's Guide to the Human Race*; interviews President Barack Obama; Stewart and Colbert hold the Rally to Restore Sanity and/or Fear in Washington, D.C.; devotes his final show of the year to the 9/11 First Responders Bill and is widely credited with its passage.

Books

Theodore Hamm. *The New Blue Media: How Michael Moore, MoveOn.org, Jon Stewart and Company Are Transforming Progressive Politics*. New York: New Press, 2008. This book describes how and why Stewart and other popular liberals have been able to influence politics.

Jason Holt. *The Daily Show and Philosophy*. Malden, MA: Blackwell, 2007. This collection of essays digs deeper into the meaning of *The Daily Show*.

Jon Stewart, Ben Karlin, and David Javerbaum. *America (The Book): A Citizen's Guide to Democracy Inaction*. New York: Warner, 2004. This colorful mock civics textbook is as full of information as jokes.

Jon Stewart, David Javerbaum, Rory Albanese, Steve Bodow, and Josh Lieb. *Earth (The Book): A Visitor's Guide to the Human Race*. New York: Busboy, 2010. This highly graphic mock textbook provides an entertaining look at the history of the planet and its human inhabitants.

Periodicals

Mike Flaherty. "Stewart Has Real Flair for the Fake News." *Variety*, January 20, 2009.

Tad Friend. "Is It Funny Yet?" *New Yorker*, February 11, 2002.

Jacob Gersman. "Why Neoconservative Pundits Love Jon Stewart." *New York*, August 9, 2009.

Jeremy Gillick and Nona Gorilovskaya. "Meet Jon Stuart Leibowitz (aka) Jon Stewart: The Wildly Zeitgeisty Daily Show Host." *Moment*, November/December 2008.

Matea Gold. "Jon Stewart Can Be Funny—Until He's Interviewing You." *Los Angeles Times*, March 14, 2009.

Jason Horowitz, Monica Hesse, and Dan Zak. "Jon Stewart, Stephen Colbert Host Rally to Restore Sanity and/or Fear on Mall." *Washington Post*, October 31, 2010.

A.J. Jacobs. "Jonny on the Spot." *Entertainment Weekly*, January 8, 1999.

Richard Morin. "Jon Stewart, Enemy of Democracy?" *Washington Post*, June 23, 2006.

Mark Peyser. "Red, White & Funny." *Newsweek*, December 29, 2003.

Gail Shister. "Young Adults Eschew Traditional Nightly News for 'The Daily Show.'" *Philadelphia Inquirer*, May 13, 2007.

Chris Smith. "America Is a Joke." *New York*, September 12, 2010.

Internet Sources

Eric Alterman. "Is Jon Stewart Our Ed Murrow? Maybe. ..." *Nation*, March 26, 2009. www.thenation.com/article/jon-stewart-our-ed-murrow-maybe.

John P. Avalon. "Stewart Rally's Point—Don't Divide Us." CNN.com, November 1, 2010. www.cnn.com/2010/OPINION/10/31/avlon.rally.sanity/index.html?iref=allsearch.

Christopher Beam. "No Joke: By Pushing for the 9/11 First Responders Health Bill, Jon Stewart Steps onto the Political Playing Field." *Slate*, December 20, 2010. www.slate.com/id/2278625.

Liz Brown. "Rally to Restore Sanity—Jon Stewart's Closing Speech (Full Text)." *Examiner.com*, October 30, 2010. www.examiner.com/celebrity-in-national/rally-to-restore-sanity-jon-stewart-s-closing-speech-full-text.

Fresh Air. "Jon Stewart: America's Ruling King of Fake News." NPR, December 28, 2010. www.npr.org/2010/12/28/132364938/jon-stewart-americas-ruling-king-of-fake-news.

Lucy Madison. "White House Lauds Jon Stewart for Pushing Passage of 9/11 Health Bill." CBSNews.com, December 21, 2010. www.cbsnews.com/8301-503544_162-20026333-503544.html.

Frances Martel. "Jon Stewart Explains the Purpose of the Rally to Restore Sanity." *Mediaite*, October 30, 2010. www.mediaite.com/tv/jon-stewart-explains-the-purpose-of-the-rally-to-restore-sanity.

Peabody Awards. "The Daily Show with Jon Stewart: Indecision 2000." www.peabody.uga.edu/winners/details.php?id=1268.

Mark A. Perigard. "Jim Cramer vs. Jon Stewart: When Blowhards Collide." *Boston Herald*, March 13, 2009. www.bostonherald.com/entertainment/television/general/view.bg?articleid=1158296.

Pew Research Center. "The Daily Show: Journalism, Satire, or Just Laughs?" May 8, 2008. http://pewresearch.org/pubs/829/the-daily-show-journalism-satire-or-just-laughs.

Stephen Thompson. "*The Daily Show*'s Stephen Colbert, Rob Corddry, Ed Helms and Mo Rocco." *A.V. Club*, January 22, 2003. www.avclub.com/articles/the-daily-shows-stephen-colbert-rob-corddry-ed-hel,13795.

Websites

The Daily Show with Jon Stewart (www.thedailyshow.com). The official home of *The Daily Show* online. The site includes a searchable archive of video clips from Stewart's first *Daily Show* to the present, as well as full episodes of recent shows, and information about Stewart and the correspondents.

"Jon Stewart," Huffington Post (www.huffingtonpost.com/news/jon-stewart). This site has a multitude of clips featuring Stewart and *The Daily Show*, a blog where readers can share thoughts on Stewart, and links to articles, videos, and information about Stewart on other sites.

Index

Randy Scherer earned his bachelor's degree in political science and creative writing from Binghamton University in 1999. He currently teaches humanities at High Tech High Media Arts in San Diego, California, where he lives with his wife and son.